A FINE LINE

A FINE LINE

DAN BURNS

CHICAGO ARTS PRESS

CHICAGO

ISBN: 978-0-9911694-2-9 (Hardcover)
ISBN: 978-0-9911694-3-6 (Trade Paperback)
Library of Congress Control Number: 2017902856

Cover art and design by Tom Sanderson
Book design by Anson Miller

Published and printed in the United States of America by
CHICAGO ARTS PRESS
www.chicagoartspress.com

Author information:
www.danburnsauthor.com
www.facebook.com/danburnsauthor/
dan@danburnsauthor.com

10 9 8 7 6 5 4 3 2 1

First Edition

As always, this one is for

Lorraine, Katie, and David

◆

And for my brother, Michael

There's a fine line between genius and insanity.
I have erased this line.

Oscar Levant

1

His gaze remained fixed on his computer screen, fingers frozen on the keyboard. An hour had passed, and the page was still blank. Nothing had come to him except a dull throb behind his eyes. He had not thought of, nor written, a single word.

A persistent knock at his door distracted him.

He looked toward the hallway through the lingering haze of smoke. The air in the room was warm and stale, and his face crinkled with displeasure. "There's no one home," he yelled.

"I am here to see a Mr. Sebastian Drake," a man said.

"Do you have an appointment?"

The door opened, and Drake heard the man snicker then step across the threshold and walk down the hallway toward him. Drake looked up and watched the man walk into the open room of his loft and up to his desk.

"I'm not interested," Drake said.

"Good day, Mr. Drake. My name is Engel, Thomas Engel."

The stranger standing before him was older, maybe fifty, Drake guessed, tall and thin with a slender face and a pencil-thin mustache. He wore a dark gray overcoat and a matching fedora. In his hand was a long umbrella. He firmly held the curved, wooden handle and bounced the metal tip on the wood floor.

What the hell?

The man did not belong in the neighborhood he was visiting, that much was certain. Drake thought he looked like he would be more comfortable walking the streets of downtown London and wondered how he had made it through the neighborhood without being assaulted.

Drake didn't have the patience or the time for the interruption. He had a book to write. "You must have the wrong address. You can let yourself out."

"I have a writing project for you, Mr. Drake."

"Is that right?" His interest was piqued, just a bit, but he remained cautious. He pointed to the chair opposite him. "Have a seat."

Engel hooked his umbrella on the back of the chair then removed his hat and set it on the desk in front of him.

"Nice hat," Drake said, an edge of sarcasm in his voice.

Engel removed his overcoat, exposing a perfectly tailored, three-piece, bespoke suit.

Drake noticed, raised his eyebrows.

Engel laid the coat over the back of the chair and sat down. He made eye contact with Drake. Neither of them said a word.

Drake broke the ice. "Can I offer you a drink?" He pulled a glass and a bottle of bourbon from the left desk drawer. He filled the glass a quarter of the way full and slid it across the desk, leaving it in front of Engel.

Engel looked at his watch.

Drake poured himself another three fingers and lit

a cigarette. He tilted his head back and blew a large plume of smoke into the air then leaned back in his chair and waited.

"It so happens that I know quite a bit about you, Mr. Drake."

"Really," Drake said. "You're not one of my crazed fans, are you?"

Engel snickered again. "Mr. Drake, let me get to the point."

"Please do."

"If I could be so blunt—you are a bit of a loser."

Drake thought about reaching across the desk to grab the intruder by the throat, but he was enjoying his cigarette and didn't feel much like moving. He took a drink instead. "That's one opinion."

"It is."

"Anyway, is that how you express your gratitude—as a fan?" Drake asked.

"Acceptance is the first step to recovery." He waited for a reaction but didn't get one. "I have been following your writing career for some time, Mr. Drake. You had a promising and successful career as a journalist but gave it up to be *creative*." Engel grinned. "You have written three novels over the last five years, and while you had some early sales success with each of your books—enough to keep your agent and publisher quite happy—I think your last royalty statement showed a total of four hundred and ninety-seven copies sold for the year. That is quite impressive," he said with his own edge of sarcasm.

"I need a new publicist."

"Your wife left you a year ago and has full custody of your children—your daughters—whom you get to see two weekends a month and on holidays. It seems she had given your new writing career more than a chance to succeed, working full-time and taking care of the children while you locked yourself in your office and toiled over your writing—your craft, as you likely call it. You are six months behind on your rent and a month behind on your alimony and child support. I suspect your bank has closed your account for lack of activity. The bookstore you run down the street is a real winner, which allows you to live in this luxury." Engel waved a hand around as if he were showing the loft to a prospective buyer.

Drake scanned the room and all its contents. His desk stood like an island in the open area of his loft, an area that served as his office, living room, and dining room, the last room description a bit of a stretch as there hadn't been much dining happening at that unadorned table and set of chairs for some months now. It wasn't perfect, but he didn't think his place was so bad.

Engel said, "You have writer's block of the worst and most detrimental sort, and your life could not be much worse. You drink too much, and at one time or another have likely considered suicide, but you know that your insurance policy will not pay after such a cowardly act. Your children would be out of luck."

Drake reached for another cigarette but found the pack empty. He opened the top desk drawer to his right, saw his spare pack, and next to it was his snub-nosed, Smith & Wesson .38-caliber revolver from the old days, his backup gun and the one he could always rely on in a pinch. He looked at it like an old friend, pondered its weight and its history. He pulled out the pack of cigarettes and lit one, then he pushed in the drawer, watching the gun disappear until the drawer closed completely.

He took a drag from his cigarette and contemplated his next move.

"You see, Mr. Drake, I am the only one who can help you, the only one who *will* help you."

"Are you queer?" Drake asked.

"Oh no, quite the contrary."

"So, how would you like to *help* me?"

"Mr. Drake, I would like to offer you a job, starting today. The job pays five thousand a week—cash—plus expenses, and promises to provide you with more than enough ideas for your next book—a successful book and a guaranteed best-seller."

"And I get to keep my clothes on?"

Engel laughed. "I assure you, Mr. Drake, the wearing of clothing is a mandatory work requirement."

Drake downed his drink, and he was surprised when Engel reached for his glass and swallowed the contents in one fluid motion. He had expected him to sip it like a fine brandy. Drake refilled both glasses then took a gulp from his own. Five thousand a week was a good sum of money, an exceptional sum given the circumstances. It was triple what he made in his best year as a journalist but short of his first year as a bestselling author, a year and a level of success that now seemed in the distant past. "Tell me more."

"I must clarify that the job I am offering is not exactly a writing project, as I may have alluded to earlier."

"Not exactly?"

"It is, more appropriately, a regular and well-paying job that will lead to a writing project."

"I'm listening."

Engel's face was stolid and fixed, like a wax figure. He sat motionless and thought about his next words. "My sister was murdered ten years ago. Today is the anniversary."

"I'm sorry," Drake said through a mouthful of smoke.

"The murderer was never apprehended, and the case is cold—dead cold. The local authorities are pretending that the case does not exist."

"Why is that?"

"It's complicated," Engel said.

"Of course it is."

Engel reached into his breast pocket and pulled out a photograph. He looked at it and sighed. He set the photograph down on the desk and slid it over.

Drake picked up the photograph. He looked down at a picture of a woman. She was young, beautiful, and proper. It looked like a school picture, likely college. She wore a white blouse, buttoned at the neck, and a navy blazer. Her golden hair was straight and hung down over her shoulders; bangs draped across her forehead. She had large, blue eyes, a sleek and sculpted nose, and high cheekbones. Her face was slender and perfect, showed a fair complexion, and Drake thought her skin looked like it was made of fine porcelain. *So innocent.*

"She was taken from this world, much too soon, Mr. Drake."

Drake leaned forward and slid the photograph back across the desk.

"Mr. Drake, I want you to look into the case and find the person who murdered my sister. I have the money, the contacts, and the political influence to make things happen."

"How much money? How much political influence?"

"More than enough."

Drake thought about what Engel had said. He thought about how he had felt just a few minutes ago and how the morning happened to take such a drastic turn. Engel had accurately assessed a good portion of his present situation, albeit a bit harshly, and Drake considered whether this proposal might be an opportunity to take a step in a different direction—the right direction, for a change. Maybe the proposal, this event, was an omen, one he should not disregard. However, he also knew from experience that opportunities in life did not come easy, and if it sounded too good to be true . . . He chewed his bottom lip. "Why don't you do it yourself?"

"That is a reasonable question, Mr. Drake. The simple answer is that I cannot, for I am very well known in town."

"I don't know you."

"Mr. Drake, I simply need someone to do the job *for* me."

"You're crazy," Drake said. "I have no experience with this type of work."

"Oh, on the contrary," Engel said. "Your early work as a journalist, when you actually worked, required the exact investigative skills that I am looking for. And while you have done a fine job of covering up your past government service, I know enough about the skills you developed through that experience to make me comfortable that you are the right person for the job."

"Then you know I could kill you, and no one would ever know."

"Mr. Drake, all I am asking is that you find my sister's murderer, and I will take care of the rest. It is a simple and straightforward proposal. I guarantee that your experience and the process will make a compelling story that you can write about." He reached into the inside breast pocket of his suit jacket and pulled out a long, thick, white envelope. He set it on the desk, laid his hand on it for just a moment, and slid it across to Drake.

Drake looked down at the envelope then up at Engel, who was smiling. Drake emptied his glass again and refilled it. He raised the bottle and tipped it toward his guest.

"I am fine, thank you," Engel said. "I only allow myself one glass of bourbon before lunch."

One glass of bourbon before lunch. Drake thought what Engel said sounded like a reasonable mantra, maybe one he himself could take on as his own—tomorrow, or next week, or the week after that—when the time was right. He leaned forward, picked up the envelope, and opened it, revealing a respectable stack of what appeared to be newly printed money, clean and crisp. He riffled through the stack of bills with his thumb—all hundreds. *Looks like five grand.*

"There are fifty, one-hundred-dollar bills," Engel said. "Feel free to count them."

Drake opened the drawer with the gun in it, closed the envelope, and tossed it in, covering up the gun. He closed the drawer. "Tell me about your sister."

Engel slid a business card across the desk. "I have a place across town. Take today off, as I am sure you think you have earned it, but please come by tomorrow evening at seven o'clock. We will talk then. And please, clean yourself up."

Drake sat back in his chair again. He looked himself over and did not see anything particularly wrong. "Do I offend you?"

Engel stood up. "Mr. Drake, you are drunk and you smell of vomit, and it is not even lunch time."

"I assure you that I can hold my liquor."

"Well, you smell of liquor, then, and smoke."

Drake nodded, conceding to the facts.

"Mr. Drake, I could lubricate my BMW with the oil slick in your hair. You are a mess, and I will not work with you in this condition." Engel reached for his coat and draped it over his arm while staring at Drake.

This guy sure can exaggerate. Drake reclined further in his chair and blew three perfect smoke rings toward the ceiling.

Engel put on his hat and grabbed his umbrella. He walked toward the door.

Drake said, "If I'm such a degenerate, such a loser, why hire me?"

Engel stopped and turned back. "Mr. Drake, you used to be a good writer, a very good writer, and could be again." He paused, straightened his posture, and with a calm but serious tone said, "And I need your help."

"What if I decide it's not my kind of project, not my cup of tea?"

"Mr. Drake, open your right-hand desk drawer."

Drake considered the request then opened the drawer. The envelope had shifted, and it rested gently against his gun. He chewed his bottom lip again then looked back up at Engel.

"Mr. Drake, you decide what is best for you." Engel walked to the doorway, seemed to pause at the threshold, then he turned and walked down the corridor to the elevator.

Drake leaned over, looked down the hallway, and saw the door wide open. "Close the door!"

There was no response, and he didn't expect one. Drake closed the desk drawer and finished his drink. He took one last drag from his cigarette and snubbed it out in the ashtray. He walked over to the door and slammed it closed then turned back around and walked to the bathroom.

Drake returned to his desk and stared at the blank page on his computer screen for another half hour. Then he typed two lines.

A SOON-TO-BE-NAMED NOVEL
By Sebastian Drake

He stared at the screen, sighed, and considered his progress. *It was something.* Then he became distracted. *Thomas Engel. Sister. Murder. Ten years ago. A job. Five grand.* Yes, he was distracted, and his creative well was bone dry. He decided to take the rest of the day off, as Mr. Engel had suggested. Maybe he *had* earned it.

2

The following morning, Drake sat alone in the coffee shop down the street from his apartment, at a square table by the front windows, staring out. The earlier buzz in the shop had quieted, and with the morning rush over, only a few solitary customers remained, nursing old coffee and wasting the morning away. The harsh sun lit most of the room and had driven the other customers away from him and into the darker rear section of the shop.

Drake wore dark sunglasses and a black suit with a black T-shirt underneath. He wore his outfit with confidence, as it sufficiently adorned his muscled, one hundred and eighty-five pound frame. His blond hair was clean but longer than he usually kept it, tucked behind his ears and touching his shoulders, and his face showed a five o'clock shadow even though it was only mid-morning. He swirled the remaining coffee in his cup while watching the traffic pass by in the street.

A middle-aged man entered the shop and made a bee-line for the counter. He gave his order to the young man at the register then shuffled down to wait for his drink. Drake thought he looked like any of a thousand others who walked the downtown streets this morning or any other morning. The uniform he wore was standard issue: dark blue suit, white shirt freshly pressed from the cleaners, red tie, and black leather shoes with a blinding shine. He worked in high finance or was maybe a lawyer. He looked like a successful businessman.

A coffee drink appeared at the counter where the man was standing. He grabbed it and walked to the front of the shop. There were twenty open tables in the front section to choose from, only one occupied. He chose the occupied table.

"Mind if I join you?" the man asked. He stood by the chair opposite Drake and waited.

Drake looked out the window and ignored the man.

"Excuse me, can I join you?"

Drake turned away from the life being played out in the street and, now agitated, looked up at the man. He scanned the room then returned his gaze to the stranger standing before him. "Are you serious?"

"You're Sebastian Drake."

"And you're interrupting. There are plenty of other tables."

Before another word was spoken, the man sat down across from Drake. He gave Drake the once-over, sizing him up, and he took a sip of his coffee while continuing to look directly at him.

Drake returned the gaze, the corner of his mouth twitching, his jaw clenched.

"You don't recognize me."

"Should I?" Drake asked, his patience thin.

"St. Peter's Elementary."

Drake expressed no recognition and did not respond.

"C'mon, we went to school together."

There was an uncomfortable moment of silence, and Drake wondered where this was going. "St. Peter's—that had to be, what, thirty years ago?" He remained cautious and tense, ready for anything.

The man sipped his coffee again then set it down. "I need to talk to you."

"I need you to move along."

"If you insist." The man reached inside his suit jacket, removed something from the inside pocket, and slid his hand down while it was still behind the veil of the lapel. He continued gazing into Drake's sunglasses. There was a loud click.

"Sebastian, please, humor me," the man said.

Drake raised a hand and reached for his sunglasses. He removed them and set them on the table. "My name is Drake, and why don't you put that toy away before you hurt yourself."

"I wouldn't call it a toy. It's a Walther PPK, .380-caliber. It's small, but it sure is effective. Given where it's aimed, I think you should be concerned."

"A Walther PPK," Drake said. "You think you're James Bond?"

The man chuckled. "You're funny. You always were. I can assure you, though, if you don't play along, you will not be laughing." He stared at Drake.

Drake stared back, unconcerned, but his eyes felt dry and irritated from the sun.

"You look terrible," the man said. "Your eyes are bloodshot and showing the effects of last night's binge. It looks like the bottle is getting the best of you."

"And you look like Ray Parsons."

Ray Parsons grinned wide. "Now that wasn't so hard. I knew you would remember me."

"How could I forget?" Drake let go of his sunglasses and reached under the table.

"What are you doing?" Parsons asked, appearing startled and uncomfortable.

"I put my finger in the barrel of your gun."

"What, are you crazy?"

"I saw it in a cartoon once. It caused the gun to backfire into the shooter's face."

"You're insane," Parsons said. "One twitch of my finger and your late-night sexual escapades are over."

"Like I said, you're Ray Parsons, and I know you don't have it in you. Besides, look around. There are witnesses. You don't go and threaten someone in a public place. Put that thing away, and tell me what's on your mind." Drake kept his finger in the barrel of the gun.

Parsons' discomfort became more evident as a heavy film of perspiration appeared on his forehead. He wiped his forehead with his free hand then wiped the hand on his pant leg. His hand was still moist, and he looked at it as though it was leprous. He raised the hand and waved it at the counter across the room.

"Hey, Timmy, be a good kid and get me a glass of water." Parsons turned back to Drake. "Where were we?"

It so happened that Timmy's name was actually Jacob. Insulted, Jacob grabbed a glass, added ice and spit, and filled the glass with water. Drake saw everything. Parsons didn't have a clue.

Jacob walked over and set the glass of water down on the table in front of Parsons. "There you are, sir." He waited a moment then returned to his station.

Parsons raised the glass to his lips.

"Don't drink that."

Parsons froze. "What?"

"Loogie," Drake said and tilted his head toward the glass. *When was the last time I said that word? When I was ten?*

Parsons lifted the glass and peered from the side. Clinging to a chunk of ice was a green-tinted garnish.

"Timmy," Parsons said through gritted teeth. He looked and saw a deserted counter, then he turned back to Drake. "Thirty years ago, you would have let me drink it . . . might even have spit in it yourself."

Drake didn't say anything, and they remained connected, finger to gun. Uncomfortable seconds passed.

"Take your jacket off and relax," Drake said. "It's a little warm in here."

Parsons stared at Drake, then looked down as if he could see through the table to the gun in his hand. Beads of sweat dripped down his forehead. He looked back up at Drake and remained still. The successful businessman was losing his edge.

"I was sorry to hear about your mother," Drake said.

Parsons thought about the words. He seemed to relax some. "I saw you at the church. You made a good effort to not be noticed, but not good enough. Why did you show?"

"I read the obituary in the newspaper. She was a good woman."

"You didn't know a thing about her."

"I used to know her," Drake said. "I used to know *you*." He removed his finger from the barrel of the gun and folded his hands in his lap.

"Are you sure you want to do that?" Parsons asked. "It was your only defense."

"I'm sure. Why are you here, Ray?"

Parsons wiped his forehead again. "You used to be so perfect, thinking you could take on the world. Now look at you. Why are *you* here?"

Drake heard the aggression in Parsons' voice, wondered if his old friend might actually take a shot at him.

Parson said, "Big shot Northwestern graduate, degree in journalism, investigative reporter for the *Chicago Tribune*—back when it was still respectable; you were a man on top of the world." He took a sip of coffee, grimacing as it went down. "The coffee here sucks." He swallowed hard a couple more times, as if trying to bury the taste. "Tell me something, Sebastian."

"Call me Drake."

"Tell me something, Drake. Where did you disappear to for those years after you graduated from Northwestern and before you started at the *Chicago Tribune*? For the life of me, I couldn't find anything about you during that time. Nothing at all. It's very strange."

"I can't remember," Drake said. "It was a long time ago. I think I recall having to go out into the world to *find myself*."

"Yeah, find yourself. Very funny. Anyway, after ten years at the *Tribune*, you decided to get creative and became a novelist. You've written three novels, each surprisingly successful but, in my opinion, not very good. I did buy a copy of each of them, though. You're welcome."

"Thanks," Drake said. "Are you going to start up my fan club?"

"This past year, your publisher dropped you, and now you live alone in a loft over on the wrong side of town. Not so perfect."

Drake thought about Thomas Engel's recent visit and found it curious that there were now two people interested in and digging into his past. His curiosity morphed into concern and heightened agitation. "What's your point?"

Parsons went for his coffee again. As he lifted the cup, Drake bolted up, sending his chair backward to the ground. He grabbed the table at the corners and rammed it into Parsons' stomach. Parsons grunted and projected a storm of spit from his lips. He dropped his coffee cup, and everything on the table flew at him. The tainted water spattered his chest, and the glass fell to the hardwood floor, bouncing a few times but remaining intact. Drake's sunglasses and empty cup followed. Drake was next to Parsons a second later, ramming his elbow into Parsons' jaw. Parsons' gun arm was pinned between the table and the back of his chair and his grip loosened, and before he could process what had just transpired, Drake laid a hand on the Walther, twisted Parsons' wrist to an unnatural angle, and took control of the gun.

"What—what did you do that for?" Parsons asked, his reaction one of stunned disbelief. He rubbed his jaw and shook off the fog in his eyes.

Drake saw the expression on his face and thought of

a Led Zeppelin song from his past: *I've been dazed and confused for so long . . .*

Parsons snapped out of it, shook his head again. "Hey, take it easy, I was just kidding."

"This gun makes me think you were quite serious," Drake said. He inspected his new acquisition and liked it. He ejected the magazine. Empty. He stuck it in his front pocket and pulled the slide back. Empty. "Well, shit."

Looking down on Ray Parsons, Drake saw a man defeated. "If you don't mind, I'll just hold on to this." He reached behind, stuck the gun in his waistband, and pulled his jacket back over it.

Parsons pushed the table away and whimpered, tried to collect himself.

Drake looked over at the counter, where Jacob had reappeared as if from thin air, towel-drying a coffee mug and smiling. Drake wondered if he had caught all of the excitement.

Jacob's boss, a short, portly man wearing a starched shirt and thick necktie covered by a dirty apron that was tied much too high above his waist, came through the storage room door. He scanned the room for the source of the disruption, stepped out from behind the counter, and hurried toward the front.

Drake watched the man approach and noticed a few other gawkers waiting in line at the counter. A man and woman in the back of the room were standing at their table, also looking at Drake and apparently uncomfortable with the situation.

"I'm the store manager here. What's going on?"

"We're fine," Drake said. "I was leaning back in my chair

and the rear legs seemed to slip out from under me. I took a pretty good fall. I think your floor is wet."

Drake bent over to pick up his toppled chair. "You should look into these chair legs." He reached down again and picked up his sunglasses and the other strewn items. He set everything on the table, adjusted it back to its original location, and sat down again opposite Parsons. He should have left but was interested in knowing how his meeting with Parsons would end. He folded his hands in his lap and stared at Parsons as though nothing had happened.

The store manager bent down, looked at the floor under and around Drake's chair, and noticed nothing unusual. "I heard the commotion from the back room. It didn't sound like anyone falling."

Parsons was rubbing his wrist. "Sir, I'm sure he's fine. Really. I'm his attorney, and I'm comfortable he will not be pressing any charges. Sorry for the commotion."

The store manager looked at Parsons, processed his words, and assessed the implication. His toughness dissipated. He looked at Drake then back at Parsons. "Well, okay then. You both have a good day." He stepped backward, keeping a watchful eye on them, and returned to his place behind the counter.

Parsons, still nursing his injury, turned to Drake and said, "Jesus Christ, you could have broken my wrist." Using his suit jacket sleeve, he wiped spit from his lips and tried to compose himself. "Where the hell did you learn to move like that?"

"Boy Scouts, eighth grade."

"What, are *you* James Bond?"

"Now I am. All I needed was the gun," Drake said. "Ray, what's on your mind?"

"You wouldn't understand."

"Let me take a shot at it. You left the old neighborhood after eighth grade and went to a private high school out east, just outside of Boston. You grew out of your uncoordinated, klutzy phase and made the high school baseball team. By senior year, you were an All-American third baseman. You must have hit the books as well, because you were accepted to Harvard, studied law, and were the editor of the *Law Review*. You were recruited by the biggest law firm here in Chicago, rose to become a full partner, and then, surprisingly, took the job as Cook County State's Attorney. And you question my career choice?"

Parsons shrugged.

"You live with your wife and two boys in a fancy house in Lake Forest. Overall, you've done quite well for yourself."

"How do you know all that?"

"I was a journalist," Drake said, "and I read the papers." They looked at each other. "I have to admit, though, I'm stumped as to what we're doing here. Is all your success too much to handle?"

"Don't play ignorant, Drake. You know exactly why I'm here."

"You'll have to enlighten me, Ray."

Parsons looked down at his red tie, now water-soaked to a cranberry hue. He shook his head, disgusted. "Everything I've done over the last thirty years, everything I've become, all the success I've realized, is because of you."

"You're welcome."

"Drake, everything I've done, I've done in spite of you."

"Sorry, you lost me again."

"Remember what good friends we were when we were younger?"

"Sure, I remember." Drake still wasn't sure where this was going.

"I looked up to you, wanted to be just like you. You were a good friend, helped me learn how to hit a fast pitch, worked me through that damn 'new math' we were learning at the time. You were popular, and I was a geek, yet you always went out of your way to include me. Then you left." Ray Parsons once again became an insecure teenager.

"Ray, I had to leave. You know that. My father received his transfer orders, and he packed us up and shipped us off to the naval base in San Diego. It wasn't the first time we moved. Three years earlier, it's what brought me here to Chicago, to the old neighborhood."

"You left me there with those animals. Without you around, everything changed. I was a social outcast. My grades suffered. I started getting my ass kicked on a regular basis again. My life became a living hell, all because of you."

"Ray, it was eighth grade. A lifetime ago."

"That may be true, but everything changed after that."

"Seems like you turned out all right."

"Once the schoolyard beatings started, my father joined in. You'd think he'd have been supportive, maybe stand up for me. No, he just called me a sissy and smacked me in the head, on a regular basis. He told me to toughen up. Hit me so hard once that he knocked me unconscious." Parsons rubbed his forehead and seemed to feel the old pain again.

"It was so bad that my mother left him. We ran, found a new place to live, a new school, a new life. My world was turned upside down. After a couple of years, things started to get better, and I vowed that I would do whatever I had to in order to get back at you, to be more successful than you."

Drake shook his head, expressing a mixture of disbelief and compassion. "You know, that's quite a grudge. You should see a therapist."

"It is, and I do," Parsons said and rubbed his jaw again. "I can't believe you hit me."

"I can't believe you pulled a gun on me," Drake said. "An empty one."

"I could never use it. I just wanted to scare you a little, make sure you listened to me." Parsons rubbed his chin and moved it back and forth to make sure his jaw was still hinged correctly. He felt his bottom lip and looked at his fingers. There was no blood.

"You could have introduced yourself politely."

"And what? You would have hugged me, told me how good it was to see me, and offered me a seat? I don't think so. You're different now."

"I'm not that different, but you're probably right." Drake spun his folded sunglasses on the table. "Look who's talking. *You're* different."

Parsons cowered a little. "I know. I have some anger management issues."

"You think? You have to let it go, Ray."

They both sat quietly, contemplating what had happened. Neither of them wanted to speak again. Enough had been said already.

Drake laughed. Parsons looked up from his lap, saw the grin on Drake's face, and laughed as well. Their laughter swelled so that everyone in the coffee shop could hear them, but they didn't care.

Drake turned back toward the counter and saw Jacob, who was drying another coffee mug and shaking his head; his smile was gone. Drake saw him mouth two words—of a derogatory nature—as he put the cup away and went about his business.

Drake and Parsons sat looking at each other, calm and quiet.

Parsons said, "I know it was a bad idea to come here. I guess I thought if I could see you, talk to you, and maybe rub a little of my success in your face, it would make me feel better. I thought it would allow me to move on. My wife and my therapist told me I needed to confront my past, my demons. Otherwise, the anger would continue to eat away at me, and I'd never be truly happy."

"How did it work out?"

"I feel worse," Parsons said. "Listen, I didn't mean what I said."

"Sure you did."

"No, I know you must be going through a tough time."

"I'm fine, I assure you," Drake said. "I'm living my dream, the life of a struggling novelist."

"Well, I guess I should be going." Parsons adjusted his tie and jacket and rose from his chair. "We should get together for a drink sometime. Who knows, maybe we could be friends again."

Drake showed no reaction at all.

"I know, don't push it," Parsons said as he hiked up his

pants and headed for the exit. He reached the door, stopped, and turned back. "Maybe I'll see you around."

Drake grinned. "It's a big city."

Parsons nodded, and he left the coffee shop. He paused at the sidewalk to take in a deep breath of the crisp morning air, and he looked up at the cloudless sky as his edge seemed to return. He crossed the front window and then was out of sight.

Once again with disbelief, Drake shook his head as he reached for his sunglasses. He put them on and returned his attention to the morning scene unfolding out in the street before him.

3

To say that the last twenty-four hours were unusual was an understatement. What were the chances of Drake running into his childhood friend, Ray Parsons, this morning? And his gun? And what about his meeting with Thomas Engel yesterday? Drake pondered these thoughts as he walked down State Street, smoking a cigarette.

On most days, Drake pursued a solitary lifestyle, one that came with his job. As a writer, he was expected to be—and needed to be—alone. He liked it that way. He had few friends, which suited him just fine, as he didn't need the additional implied responsibility or expected complications. Since his divorce, the law kept the interaction with his ex-wife and children to a minimum. There were no other distractions. How strange it seemed to Drake that on each of the last two days, he had received a visit from two quite different and unusual people, both of whom had delved into his past. What were the odds that he would have that much interpersonal contact in such a short time? Not very good. It was a long shot, and Drake thought what had happened the last two days was odd—very odd.

His phone rang, and he pulled it from his pocket. He

glanced at the caller-ID on the display and saw that it was his literary agent, Barbara Sellers. She had helped him to get his three prior books sold and published and was the one person who realized that Drake was not meeting his full writing potential. She was now the only one who truly cared about his career, maybe even more than he did. His ex-wife, Karen, used to care more than anyone, but Drake felt she had given up on him. Barbara knew Drake was in a slump and felt the need to push him, hard and on a regular basis, to deliver his next novel. She was in New York, her agency residing in a fancy office on Fifth Avenue, but she called him often to provide the necessary nudge, support, and inspiration, whether Drake wanted it or not.

Drake thought about the last time he had seen Barbara. She was a professional, stylish, and attractive woman who maintained a classic, voluptuous body that people of both sexes could appreciate. She wore her hair long and colored auburn and possessed a pair of mesmerizing green eyes. She was about his age, and when they were seen together, Drake knew it was conceivable that people might assume that they had been or were in an intimate relationship. However, intimacy was not a feeling Drake shared regarding Barbara. He liked her and enjoyed spending time with her, but it ended there. It was just business.

Drake stopped in front of one of the neighborhood liquor stores. Sliding metal grates covered the windows and door. He peered through the window and listened; it was dark and silent inside.

He stepped into the doorway alcove and answered the call. "Yeah."

"Drake, that's no way to answer a call from your favorite agent," Barbara said. Her voice was loud and somewhat gravelly, like the actress Kathleen Turner, Drake thought, and she was seductive in her speaking style and approach.

"You're my only agent," Drake said.

"I'm glad you realize that, darling."

Drake remained silent. It was still too early in the morning to be interested.

"Are you there?"

"What can I do for you, Barbara? I'm busy."

"Working on your new—" she said. "Sorry, I'm getting ahead of myself. Drake, the question is, 'what can I do for you?'"

"Really," Drake said, surprised.

"Yes, darling, I've been racking my brain day and night for an idea to get someone to bite on your new book."

"And?"

"I spoke with Random House, and they're ready to sign."

Now, Drake was interested. "Really," he said again.

"Don't sound so surprised. You have a good agent, and I just happen to have a few friends who like me, if you know what I mean. An editor at Random House, Larry Davis, and I go way back."

"You mean you put yourself out, there, for me?"

"And for me," Barbara said.

Drake could have sworn he heard her purr. "So, what's the deal?"

"A twenty-five thousand dollar advance and our standard royalty rate."

"Sounds a little low."

"Compared to zero?"

Drake was silent as he considered her point. The advance was less than what he had received for his first book, a deal which he lucked out on at a time when the publishing world was different, more interested in taking chances and spending money to acquire new talent, but it was more than what he had received for his last two books. His publisher had told him that, given the success of his first book, he'd make more money with a higher royalty rate, which didn't quite pan out—not yet, at least. So, twenty-five grand was a respectable number given the circumstances and the current state of his new book.

"Drake?"

"What's the initial print run?" Drake asked.

"It doesn't matter. Take the money. Let the publisher worry about how many copies to print and how to sell the book."

"What's the catch?" There was always a catch.

"What catch?" Barbara said sounding surprised.

"They're going to pay me twenty-five grand for nothing but a title page and my stellar publishing history?"

"You told me you were further along."

"Revision is brutal."

"It doesn't matter," she assured him. "Your previous books sold well, made your old publisher a lot of money. The only reason they let you go is because of their merger and desire to cut back on genre fiction. Anyway, Larry at Random House is a big fan of yours and loves a good mystery novel. He knows your sales numbers and wants to see you get to the next level. I shared the synopsis for your new book, your outline, and myself with him. It was enough, more than enough. Just get started. The story will come."

"When are they expecting it—the final manuscript?"

Barbara was silent.

"Barbara?"

"In a month."

Drake laughed. He looked up and down the street to see if anyone was within earshot. He was alone.

"They want it for their spring catalog," she said. "They had an author who dropped the ball, who is not able to deliver as promised. They're in a bind, and one author's misfortune is another author's opportunity—your opportunity. Larry's ass is in a pinch, and he's not going to tell the board of directors that their spring releases will be one short. You're going to make sure of that. I promised Larry that you'd have your book ready by the end of next month, for submission to his editing team, so you have a little bit more than five weeks. Feel better?"

"No."

"Drake, I put my ass on the line for you. Do not let me down."

"Impossible," Drake said.

"I thought you were going to say, 'I'm good, but I'm not that good.'"

"You know me well."

"I should. I do," she said. "You'll have your check by the end of the week. That'll ease your mind some."

"What about the contract?"

"Larry let me sign for you, in good faith. We'll formalize everything later. Just get going."

Drake was still considering the word *check*. "I'll think about it."

"Drake, darling, this is a good deal, a very good deal. You're a writer, and all you have to do is what you're best at. All you have to do is write. Just write."

"Yeah, just write."

"Listen, Drake, darling, I have to go. Keep a look out for the check, and I'll call you in a week. Okay?"

Drake didn't say anything. He was still processing the moment.

"Drake?"

"Thanks, Barbara."

"In a week?"

"In a week," Drake said. He put the phone away then lit another cigarette, stepped out from the doorway, and continued down the street.

* * *

The South Loop area of Chicago was an urban melting pot of people, culture, commerce, and residential development. A once-thriving area with factories, storage facilities, and businesses a hundred years ago, the area fell on hard times as the country moved to a more service-based economy. A period of desertion and decline in the seventies and eighties had followed the prior decades of growth and prosperity, to a point where people knew the area more for the crimes that took place in and among the abandoned and neglected buildings.

Over the last fifteen years, the area had experienced a resurgence of growth, development, and renewed prosperity.

The revitalization was widespread but spotty, in some cases "here today and gone tomorrow," and you could find a building of renovated loft condominiums, with two bed-room units going for $300 thousand and up, situated right next to a vacant retail building that served, unbeknownst to the authorities, as a crack house. It would take some years for the current grand vision for the neighborhood to come to fruition.

Drake stopped in front of an old, two-story building in a previously industrial, now commercial area of the neighborhood. It was a fixture in the not-quite-gentrified area just down the street from where he lived. The building housed a retail space on the first floor that had a sign on the window: RETAIL SPACE AVAILABLE. Drake looked at the sign and shook his head. The sign had been there for a year now since the last tenant, a husband-and-wife team who managed a yoga center, had moved out. Above him was an awning over the building entrance, which read: THE BOOK LOFT. He reached for the heavy wooden door, opened it, and entered the small lobby.

Drake crossed the mosaic tile floor and stepped into an old elevator—which bounced some as he entered—and pulled the sliding cage door closed. He pressed a button on the panel to his right, and the elevator slowly ascended. Cables stretched and creaked, and a motor turned and rumbled at the base of the shaft below him. He rode the elevator up to the second floor, where it screeched to a stop. He slid the cage door of the elevator open and stepped out, sliding the door closed behind him.

Before him was his bookstore, his pride and joy—ranked

in importance third after his daughters and his published books—and he stood for a moment to appreciate the sight. The loft area in front of him was one large room of two thousand square feet. The room had brick walls, fifteen-foot ceilings with exposed timber trusses, rough-hewn hardwood floors, and overflowing bookcases in every direction. The room was bright with natural light, silent, and devoid of any customers.

To his right was an immense oak checkout counter, like you might find at an old general store, and sitting behind the counter was his store manager, Rita. She had a medium build, short dark hair, and an unadorned, pretty face framed by rectangular, black-rimmed glasses. She looked much younger than her thirty-two years might suggest and was the cute-and-bookish librarian type. She was soft-spoken and forever loyal to her employer.

"Why, hello," Rita said. "I wasn't expecting you this early, or today, for that matter."

"Looks like we're packing them in." Drake looked around at the empty room.

"It's early. They'll start trickling in during the lunch hour."

Drake wanted to believe her but expressed concern.

"Don't worry," she said. "They'll come."

Drake walked into the room a few feet farther and continued his visual inspection. "How much did we take in yesterday?"

"A little over one-fifty."

Shaking his head, he said, "What am I doing?"

"What?" Rita asked.

Drake turned around. "What are you doing today?"

She pointed to a stack of boxes by the bare, hazy windows. "That's the acquisition we took in over the weekend. It's a pretty nice collection: lots of rare volumes, some signed, some leather. I'd like to get them into inventory and in the display cases. Customers can't buy the books if they can't see them."

"That makes sense."

"It was a steal for only fifteen hundred."

He winced.

"What?"

"Nothing." He scanned the room, distracted. "Anything left in the till?"

"A few hundred. You want me to hold off on lining up further acquisitions? I can do that if you'd like."

"You know me. I can't say 'no' to a good book or a good deal." He walked over to the counter, pulled out his newly acquired envelope of cash, and wondered if it might be too soon to reduce its size. He thumbed off ten one-hundred-dollar bills and handed them to Rita.

"My goodness," she said, surprised. "Have you been doing something naughty?"

"I'm prostituting myself."

"Really?"

Drake shook his head. "No. But I did just get hired for a short term research project that happens to pay pretty well."

"Research? Can I help? Tell me about it."

Drake shot her a serious stare, narrowed his eyes.

"I know. Then you'd have to kill me," she said.

"I'll fill you in when it's over. How's that?"

"Promise?"

Drake had already turned away and was scanning the room again, not sure what he was looking for but seeking some revelation.

"Drake?"

"Yeah, I promise," he said. "Listen, I have a meeting later with the client who hired me, and I need to prepare a little."

"A nap?" She knew him well.

"Amongst other things. Can you handle everything here?"

"I always do."

"You do, and thanks." Drake walked toward the elevator. As he slid the cage door open and walked in, he said, "See you tomorrow?"

Rita, her chin resting on a palm with an elbow on the desk, turned toward him. A faint and understanding smile remained. "Yep."

Drake closed the cage door, hit a button, and the elevator descended to the lower level.

4

Within the city boundaries of Chicago, there was money and then there was serious money, and the serious money found its way to the quiet, tree-lined streets in the Gold Coast area just north of downtown. It was early evening, and Drake walked the Gold Coast streets not because of his accumulated wealth, of which there was none, but because he was called to the area as a guest.

After some reading back at his apartment, a half a pack of cigarettes, a quick nap, and a hurried dinner, he had gone out for his evening appointment. As usual, he walked to his destination. He didn't have a car, didn't need one, and couldn't afford one. This part of town was different than where he lived in the South Loop. It was quieter, safer, more pleasant, and life carried on without any interaction with the larger city's more dangerous and undesirable elements. Drake enjoyed the walk, for he did not need to be cautious or even cynical. He slowed his pace and observed the aged but uniquely designed buildings as he passed them. Many of the buildings were constructed during the same time period, but each one reflected the architect's and original owner's specific design choices. Overall, everything seemed so much grander: the stone and brick, the windows, the entry doors, the wrought iron, even the trees. He pulled the business card out of his pocket, read it, and walked ahead a half block more until he came to his destination.

Drake stood in front of an elegant, three-story fortress built from large granite blocks in rich and complementary shades of gray and red. The roof was tiled with green slate and framed with blue-green copper gutters. Cut out of the facade were two pillared balconies, one each on the first and second floors, large enough to accommodate a good-sized dinner party. In front of him was a six-foot-tall wrought iron fence, and to the left of the gate was an intercom box. He pressed the button and waited.

His eyes traveled up the front limestone stairs to an entryway carved out of a three-story stone turret. Every window in the turret had a curved-stone arch above it, an architectural detail Drake imagined was quite expensive to create, adding up the labor necessary to lay the stone and the cost of the custom window. He gazed up at the second floor window of the turret, which was just tall and wide enough to frame the shadow of a person looking down at him.

A woman's voice coming from the intercom speaker broke his concentration. "Hello, can I help you?"

Drake stepped forward and leaned in toward the box. "Sebastian Drake. I'm here to see Thomas Engel."

The box remained silent for a few seconds, then the locking mechanism of the gate buzzed. Drake pushed the gate forward and it swung open, allowing him to enter the small front yard. He closed the gate behind him and walked up the stairs and into the curved opening in the turret. He approached a large door made with wood from an old and distant forest.

He waited for a moment, his hands clasped behind his back as he studied the door and the small, iron-caged cutout at eye level. Impatient, he leaned forward and raised an arm to knock, and at the same time, the door opened, gliding on its hinges.

An older, demure woman stood before him, smiling. Drake returned the smile and thought the woman seemed quite proper, yet maybe a little pretentious in her stance. He figured she was about sixty and certainly the wife of Thomas Engel. She was short, thin, and handsome. Her gray-streaked hair was pulled back, and she wore a dark and conservative pantsuit.

"Mr. Drake, please come in. I'm Marion Engel. Thomas is expecting you."

Drake stepped into the foyer, and she closed the door behind him. He walked in a bit farther and looked around, impressed.

"Please excuse me," Marion said. "I was upstairs putting some things away." She looked at Drake, intrigued, as a zoologist might observe a new species of animal. "May I take your coat?"

"Thank you." Drake removed his black trench coat, revealing a dark gray suit, white shirt, and royal blue tie.

She took the coat, draped it over her arm, and stood, waiting and still smiling.

Drake wondered what she was waiting for. "You have a beautiful home."

"Why, thank you."

"I was expecting the butler," Drake said.

She laughed and raised a hand to cover her mouth. She appeared to be a little embarrassed. "Mr. Drake, you're funny." She lowered her hand. "No, there are no butlers here, no servants. Thomas and I are the only ones who roam these halls."

Drake nodded and looked around again. "Is Mr. Engel available?"

Before she could respond, Drake heard footsteps across the ceiling above him. He looked up. The footsteps continued and proceeded down what sounded like a long hallway then descended a flight of stairs. At the landing of the substantial mahogany staircase before him, Drake watched as Thomas Engel came into view. He noticed Engel's attire— dark slacks, a cardigan sweater, a crisp collared shirt, and a bow tie—and felt the wardrobe appropriately matched the man.

"Mr. Drake, how nice of you to come by," Engel said. He continued down the stairs and walked across the foyer to where Marion and Drake stood. "Marion, I see you have already met Mr. Drake."

"I have."

Engel shook hands with Drake. "Thank you for coming."

"My pleasure."

"Marion, we will be upstairs in the library," Engel said. He leaned over and kissed her on the cheek. She beamed like a young girl on a first date.

Engel said to Drake, "Please, come this way."

Drake bowed his head toward Marion. "It was a pleasure to meet you."

"And you," Marion said, and she turned and walked down the hallway with Drake's coat.

Engel and Drake watched her for just a moment, then Engel reached for Drake's elbow and extended a hand to show him the way. They walked up the stairway to the second floor. At the top of the landing was a long hallway that split and went off in opposing directions. Directly in front of them was a pair of eight-foot-tall doors. Engel took hold of both door handles and pushed the doors open wide in a grand presentation. He stepped aside. "After you."

Drake entered the room and observed the expansive space: a forty-by-forty-foot room, he guessed, with a twenty-foot-high ceiling. The walls were lined with built-in walnut bookcases, and every inch of every shelf held a book. As he walked, he noticed that many of the volumes were leather-bound, aged, and gilt-edged. The continuous lines of the bookcases were broken only by the entry doors he had just passed through, a set of windows at the far end of the room, and a massive stone fireplace in the corner, where a fire was raging. In the center of the room were matching leather sofas, which faced each other, and an elegant, rectangular coffee table was set between them.

"Nice room," Drake said.

"Please, will you have a seat?"

Drake began a self-guided tour of the room, scanning the bookcases. At the third bookcase in and on his left, he spotted a book that captured his attention. He stopped, pulled the book from the shelf, and inspected it, as if holding a new archaeological find.

"Something of interest?" Engel asked.

Drake turned toward Engel. "Ray Bradbury's first book, *Dark Carnival*, first edition, signed. Very nice."

"Thank you."

"You don't seem the type," Drake said.

"Nor you."

Drake put the book back into its space on the shelf and walked on.

"It appears we have similar interests, Mr. Drake, that we are more alike than you might think."

Drake looked at Engel, his disbelieving stare conveying *I don't think so.*

"Mr. Drake, I would like you to have that book, as a gift, from one book lover to another."

"I don't think so."

"Will you reconsider? Your acceptance would please me and would help to get our relationship off to a good start."

"There is no relationship."

Engel let the comment pass. He walked over to one of the sofas and sat down.

Drake took his time walking the full perimeter of the room, and when finished, he walked over to the other sofa and sat opposite Engel. They stared at each other. The room was eerily quiet except for the crackling wood in the fireplace.

"Can I offer you a drink? Bourbon?" Engel asked. He motioned toward the silver tray, the bottle of bourbon, and the two rocks glasses on the table.

Drake folded his hands in his lap. He showed no expression but glanced at the bottle on the tray and recognized it: Pappy Van Winkle, twenty-three-year-old bourbon.

A similar bottle was offered to Drake some years back, a gift from his publisher after the release of his first book, and he remembered the taste, the resulting high, and the subsequent hangover. "I'm fine."

"No? Too early?"

"I thought I might take a break today," Drake said.

Engel appeared surprised and somewhat impressed. He sat back, folded his hands in his lap—mimicking Drake—and studied him. "I like your suit."

Drake sighed, annoyed.

"And you clean up nicely."

"Why don't we get to the point, the reason why I'm here," Drake said.

"Which is what?"

"Tell me about your sister."

"Very well." Engel paused, contemplative. "Mr. Drake, why are you here?"

"I had nothing better to do tonight, the weather is nice, and it seemed like a good night for a walk."

"I see. So, let us talk about your new job."

"I haven't accepted yet," Drake said.

"But you accepted payment."

"I can return it."

"Can you? All of it?"

Drake didn't respond.

Engel leaned forward and poured a drink for himself. He stood up and took a sip of the bourbon then walked away, obtained a bit of distance, and turned back toward Drake. "Mr. Drake, I would like to tell you about the murder of a young woman by the name of Sarah Mitchell."

"Your sister," Drake said.

"No, not exactly."

"Then you lied?"

"Not exactly."

Drake stood up. His patience was thinning. "I've already had enough."

"Mr. Drake, please. Sit down. I meant no harm. I needed to get your attention."

Drake remained standing, glaring at Engel, his brow furrowed.

"Sarah Mitchell was engaged to my younger brother," Engel said. "They were to be married upon his return from military deployment. Marines. Unfortunately, he never returned, alive that is."

Drake sat down. "I'm sorry."

"Thank you," Engel said, as he seemed to reflect on his thoughts and words. "She was a wonderful young woman: beautiful, talented, only eighteen years old." He paused, again contemplative, and his expression changed to one of disappointment. "I promised my brother that I would look after her while he was away. I did not keep my promise."

Drake looked at the bottle on the table. He thought about reaching for it.

"Sarah was murdered while my brother was off on a deployment. He never knew. She was murdered, and then he was killed three days later when he stepped on a roadside bomb. I vowed to do whatever was necessary to find the person responsible for her murder. I owe that much, to her and to my brother."

Drake reached for the bottle and poured himself a drink.

He sat back and raised the glass to his lips, smelled the rising vapors first, then took a long swallow. His tongue tingled as he savored the taste, detecting flavors of wood, spice, and caramel. He stared at Engel. "Let's start at the beginning."

"Very well. Ten years ago, this month, the severed hand of Sarah Mitchell was found on the grounds of the Lincoln Park Conservatory."

"The botanical garden," Drake said, "over by the Lincoln Park Zoo, not too far from here."

"Yes, that is correct." Engel said. "Her body was never recovered."

"There was an investigation, I assume?"

"Of course. I am not surprised that you do not remember. You were off on your own deployment at the time." Engel looked at Drake.

Drake nodded.

"The case was hot for six months and kept open for two years, at which time it went cold, ice cold. Everyone lost interest: the public, the police, the politicians, the FBI, everyone. Since that time, I have pursued the investigation myself, in a manner of speaking. Over the years, let me just say that I have had the opportunity to acquire the resources necessary to heat the case up once again."

"Resources?"

"Yes, Mr. Drake. People, connections, money, and technology . . . each of which has, in some way, provided me with access to the data, information, and facts needed to help solve this murder. And I have just acquired a missing piece of the puzzle, a piece shared with me from a most surprising and interesting source, a person you could never imagine coming forth to help."

"Who is that?"

"That is not important right now."

"Do you know who killed her?"

"No," Engel said.

"Well then." Drake was losing interest.

Engel walked over to Drake and set his glass down on the tray. "Mr. Drake, can I show you something?"

"Sure."

Engel walked toward the door. Drake emptied his glass, set it down, then stood up and followed Engel down the hallway.

5

After Engel had visited him in his apartment the day before, Drake was not quite sure what to make of his new acquaintance. Now, Drake grasped all of Engel's obvious qualities: mature, distinguished, wealthy, determined, educated, and intelligent, the last quality dependent on the individual and which does not necessarily go along with being educated. Engel seemed to have it all. However, Drake also sensed an underlying, mysterious quality about the man that he could not quite discern. He sensed that Mr. Engel was not all he projected himself to be. Drake considered his assessment further as he followed Engel down the hall from the library to the next door on the right.

As they approached the doorway, Engel said, "Mr. Drake, how is the weather outside?"

"Clear and cool. A nice, fall day."

To the right of the doorway, mounted to the wall at eye level, there was a black, glass panel, about twelve inches square. Engel stepped forward and the panel lit up, changing from black to white. He stood before the panel, quiet and motionless, and stared at it.

Drake looked over Engel's shoulder at the glass panel, which displayed:

PRIMARY SUBJECT ACCESS GRANTED.
SECONDARY SUBJECT EVALUATION PENDING . . .

Drake was impressed. "Retina scans?"

"Yes," Engel said. "Along with facial composition matching and voice recognition." He stepped aside. "Would you mind stepping forward?"

Drake stood before the panel. "Need me to say anything?"

"Your voice pattern has already been captured."

Drake saw the glass panel go blank for just a second, then he saw:

SECONDARY ACCESS GRANTED.

He heard a loud click at the door lock, followed by the sounds of multiple bolts sliding within the door.

Engel opened the door and walked in. The lights in the room came on automatically. Drake followed him inside.

They stood in a room about half the size of the library. The walls were covered with rich walnut panels, and a large glass video panel covered most of the wall in front of them. There was a long and elaborate desk—made of the same walnut wood—that spanned the width of the room. The desk was covered with a dozen sleek computers, all dark and quiet.

Engel walked forward to the desk, and the wall and computer panels lit up.

"A war room," Drake said.

"In a sense."

Drake stood beside Engel, assessing and evaluating the technology and trying to absorb and make sense of the content displayed on the screens. To the layperson, the moving and continually refreshed content would likely mean nothing, might even be overwhelming or distracting, but Drake was absorbing the information and putting the pieces together.

Engel turned toward Drake and watched him, trying to get a sense of his understanding. He returned his gaze to the video panel on the wall. "Mr. Drake, the main display in front of you reflects the results of my work so far: everyone and everything that is, in some way, connected to the Sarah Mitchell murder case."

Drake observed a complex collection of names, headshots, maps, and connecting lines on the wall display. "You've been busy."

Engel said, "I have done the leg work. I need you to take it from here. I have the plan, the contacts, and the information you need."

"It looks like you've managed just fine on your own. What do you do for a living?"

"I am a philanthropist."

"Of course you are."

"Mr. Drake, the investigation needs a personal touch— *your* personal touch. I have connected the dots I know, yet I fear there are still some dots that are missing. I need you to help me uncover the missing pieces."

Drake glanced down and saw two leather portfolios on

the desk. Engel picked up the rightmost one and handed it to him. He opened the portfolio and found an ultra-thin computer tablet display. He inspected the tablet. Based upon the minimal thickness of the device—less than an eighth of an inch, Drake guessed—he was looking at a device that incorporated technology not yet available in the commercial or retail market.

"The device contains everything you will need," Engel said. "Who to speak with, sequence of events and actions, background information, everything."

Drake closed the portfolio and handed it back to Engel. "I'm not much of a computer guy."

It appeared that Engel had expected such a response. He set the portfolio down, picked up the other one, and handed it to Drake. "A traditionalist. I respect that."

Drake opened the second portfolio and found a lengthy document, crisply typeset on high quality paper. He leafed through the pages, scanned the content, and closed the portfolio.

Engel said, "I can assume that you will appropriately secure the information I provide you and keep it strictly confidential."

Drake nodded.

"Very well." Engel reached down and pulled out a drawer from beneath the desk counter. Inside the drawer was a rectangular, black box that looked like it was made of onyx, which he lifted up and presented to Drake.

"A gift?" Drake asked.

"So to speak," Engel said as he handed the black box to Drake.

Drake put the portfolio under his arm and grabbed hold of the box, felt its smooth and cold surface. He lifted the lid and stared at the contents.

"Are you still carrying your old Walther pistol, Mr. Drake?"

Drake said nothing.

"No? Don't tell me you changed to a gun that is more, how shall I say, progressive . . . more high tech? I thought you were a traditionalist."

"I don't carry any more."

"Of course," Engel said. "However, in case you should reconsider, the thirty-two-caliber bullets for your Walther are on the left and just as you like them. Nine-millimeter rounds are on the right. Just in case you decide to join us in the current decade with your choice of gun."

Drake looked at the bullets, inspected them closely, then he closed the lid on the box. "What makes you think I need these?"

"Just a hunch."

"I can get my own ammunition, thank you."

"Can you? These rounds are quite unique. They were engineered by some very intelligent and secretive people for maximum velocity, razor-sharp accuracy, high impact, and, best of all, they are absolutely untraceable."

"Everything is traceable," Drake said.

Engel laughed. "Mr. Drake. Please understand that I have done my homework and that I know everything about these bullets . . . and about your past."

"I doubt it."

"These rounds are familiar to you, yes?"

Drake said nothing.

"Of course they are familiar. They're yours."

"I don't know what you're talking about."

Engel smiled.

"Where did you get them?" Drake asked.

"That is not important. What is important is that I acquired them, and now I want you to have them."

Drake stared at the closed box as his mind replayed scenarios and circumstances from the past, carried them forward to the present time, and tried to make sense of the corresponding facts, possibilities, and logic. *No way.*

Engel was staring at him, and Drake wondered if Engel saw the concentration in his expression and realized that he was putting the pieces together.

"Please, Mr. Drake, take them. They may come in handy."

Drake considered Engel's statement, further assessed the situation, and conceded. "Very well."

"So, we have an agreement, Mr. Drake? You will take the assignment . . . and the money?"

"Sure," Drake said, without hesitation or emotion. He tucked the black box next to the portfolio under his arm.

"Excellent," Engel said, now pleased. "I believe you have everything you need, but if not, all you have to do is ask."

Drake walked toward the door.

"Mr. Drake."

Drake turned around.

"Could I interest you in joining us for a late supper? Marion has prepared one of her specialties: roasted quail."

"Thank you, but I have leftovers waiting for me at home."

"Very well then."

"I'll see myself out. Please give my regards to Mrs. Engel," Drake said, and he left the room.

* * *

After leaving Engel's home, Drake walked the two or so miles of city streets back to his South Loop neighborhood. The evening hour was getting late, and the streets were quiet. Drake enjoyed several cigarettes—always Marlboro Lights—as he walked and thought about the situation, the assignment, he was now immersed in. He thought more about his new acquaintance and employer, Mr. Thomas Engel, and how some details of the mystery surrounding Engel were coming more into focus. At the same time, the overall mystery about Engel himself was becoming more disconcerting. Engel was not what he seemed or appeared to be.

At the north edge of the South Loop area, Drake walked by a pub and stopped to glance through the front window, looking past the illuminated, neon, Old Style sign. The pub was empty, no one visible except the bartender, so he went inside for a drink.

6

Drake awoke early the next morning at six, which surprised him since he had only four hours of sleep. After a few beers at the bar, he had gone home and stayed up late, thinking about his meeting with Engel and trying to piece together the background and true motives of his new employer. A philanthropist. *I don't think so.* His mind had worked overtime, and because he decided to forgo his normal late evening bourbon sedative, sleep had not come easily.

On the positive side, he did not have a hangover. He jumped up from bed, showered, dressed, and went to the kitchen to make breakfast. All the while, his mind was still racing. *What the hell happened last night? Who is this guy, Engel? Where did he get those bullets? What does he know, and how did he find out? Who does he know, and what is he really capable of? Who was his new source, the person I could never imagine?* He sat down at his desk, ate a piece of toast, and washed it down with a cup of black coffee. Black was the only way he could drink it, unless it had a kick—of bourbon.

He opened the leather portfolio Engel had given him then glanced at the black box just next to it on his desk. He leafed through the pages once again, this time slower, more attentive and deliberate, and he read and concentrated on every word. As he read, he made several notes on the once-perfect pages. When he had finished with the final page, he closed the portfolio and sat back in his chair, his elbows on the armrests and his folded hands up at his mouth.

One thing was clear to Drake: he had a lot of questions that needed answers, and he knew the only way to untie the knot in his stomach was by searching for and obtaining those answers—sooner than later.

* * *

Drake took a taxi to the 18th District Police Station on North Larrabee. He decided on the taxi over the forty-five minute walk through the city, but given the time of morning and the rush of cars and people on their way to work, the taxi ride did not save him much time. He learned from Engel's notes that the 18th was the station that initially handled the Sarah Mitchell case, and Engel felt it was the best place to start. Drake had no reason to disagree.

After exiting the car, Drake stood in front of the station and scanned the length of the property. The building was a block wide and two stories tall, a boxy and typical-looking municipal building constructed of brick and glass. The face of the building appeared in three sections—brick-glass-brick— with the middle all-glass section making up the entryway and fronting a two-story atrium. There was sparse landscaping, and Drake thought it odd that there were three large trees poking up out of grates set within the sidewalk, which was constructed of concrete and pavers. The only remarkable feature of the building Drake noticed was a double row of staggered black and white blocks, on the right section of the facade, which replicated the band on the department-issued Chicago police officer hat.

Drake entered the building through a revolving door, passed through a small vestibule and another glass door, and approached the watch commander's desk. Behind the desk was an older officer, male, about fifty-five years of age, and wide, wearing the force's standard-issue sky-blue shirt. Drake figured the officer had had a good run, was nearing the end of his career, and was riding out his time in his current quiet and unthreatened role.

The watch commander looked up from his desk.

"I'm here to see Detective Hartman," Drake said.

The man seemed inconvenienced. "Is he expecting you?"

"No, but he'll want to see me."

"Your name?"

"Mr. Drake."

The watch commander glared at Drake suspiciously. He picked up the phone and dialed an extension. He waited, then said into the phone, "Hartman, there's a Mr. Drake here to see you." He listened then glanced up at Drake, grinning. "Sebastian?"

"That's right."

Back into the phone, the watch commander said, "That's him." He listened again and chuckled. He looked at Drake and said, "Have a seat. He'll be right up." It seemed as though Drake had brought a little sunshine into the man's otherwise dismal day.

Drake walked over to a wood bench on the far wall where a handcuffed teenager was sitting. They assessed but did not acknowledge each other. Just as Drake was about to sit, Detective Mike Hartman rounded a corner just down the hallway to the left and walked into the room. He was an imposing figure at six-foot-two and a good two hundred and fifty pounds. His suit coat strained from the mass of flesh, muscle, and bone underneath it.

"Well, well, I don't believe it," Hartman said. He approached Drake and extended a hand.

Drake stepped forward, cracked a smile, and shook his hand. "Mike."

"Sebastian," Hartman said, grinning.

Drake glared at him.

"Yeah, yeah, I remember. You never quite cared for that name, as I recall."

"Drake is fine."

"How long's it been?" Hartman asked.

"It's been a while."

"I'll say. You keep in touch with anyone from the old neighborhood?"

"No."

Hartman nodded, seemed to expect the answer. "A bunch of us met up at the old bar, The Pumping Company, a couple of months ago. I ran into Carrie Jenkins. Remember her? She was asking about you. She's still quite a package. Told her I hadn't seen or heard from you in fifteen years. She seemed disappointed."

"I've been busy," Drake said.

"Yeah, sure. So, what can I do for you?"

"Can we talk, somewhere private?"

"Sure. C'mon, we'll go down the hall to a conference room."

Hartman led Drake down a long hallway to the third door on the right.

As they entered the room, Drake winced at the harsh light and was not impressed with the room decor: flat white suspended tile ceiling, beige walls, and industrial vinyl tiles of a similar color on the floor. Hartman circled around and sat at a laminated conference table with an unnatural brown color, which was large enough to accommodate a meeting for six. Drake sat at the closer middle chair, across from Hartman.

"I need your help," Drake said.

"You? As I recall, you never wanted or needed help from anyone."

"I'd like to get access to one of your old case files."

"And why is that?"

"It's a case that's been cold for eight years," Drake said. "I've been hired to look into it."

Hartman appeared perplexed. "I thought I heard that you're a writer."

"I am."

"Then I think I'll have to decline."

"Maybe you remember the case: Sarah Mitchell, daughter of the famed Senator Mitchell of Illinois, murdered, her severed hand found over by the Lincoln Park Conservatory. The body was never recovered."

"I remember," Hartman said, appearing to recall the case. He sat up straighter, was a little more interested. "I was on patrol that day, was one of the first to respond. Chief Peters— he was Detective Peters at the time—led the investigation. Why do you care?"

There was a knock at the door. They remained locked in on each other.

"Come in," Hartman said.

The door opened, and a woman looked in. She stood in the doorway, her hands on her hips, looking first at Hartman and then at Drake.

"Angie, c'mon in. This is Sebastian Drake. He's a friend from the old neighborhood." To Drake he said, "This is my partner, Detective Angie Parker."

Drake knew Detective Parker had been Hartman's partner for the last eighteen months, replacing his previous partner who was killed in the line of duty. She was thirty-four years old.

Drake looked at her and could tell from her stance and expression that, while small in stature, she was confident and strong. But he also sensed a trace of vulnerability in her eyes. She was beautiful, physically fit, and dressed in a navy pantsuit and blue, collared blouse. Her long, curly, black hair framed her smooth, alabaster complexion.

Drake stood and extended a hand. "Detective Parker."

She grasped Drake's hand and shook it once. She looked into his eyes for a long moment, expressionless, as he held on. "Mr. Drake." He let go, and she walked around the table and sat next to Hartman.

"It seems Mr. Drake here was hired to look into an old case of ours," Hartman said. "The Sarah Mitchell murder that went cold eight years ago."

Parker looked at Hartman, then at Drake, inquisitively. "I think I know you," she said. "Are you Sebastian Drake, the writer?"

"You know of him?" Hartman asked. He acted and sounded surprised.

"Yeah. A friend of mine recommended his last book to me. It wasn't bad, except that everyone died in the end."

Hartman said, "Drake, this is quite a day for you, getting to meet the one person who read a book of yours." He laughed.

The comment came across as a good-natured but still pointed ribbing from Hartman, just like in the old days, Drake remembered, when it seemed Hartman was always trying to put somebody down to make himself feel better about what were likely his own inadequacies. Drake considered the possibility that Hartman hadn't changed too much in all the years that had passed.

"I'm honored," Drake said.

"So, if you're a writer, why would someone hire you to look into a cold murder case?" Parker asked. She stared at him, waiting for an answer.

Drake didn't respond.

There was another knock on the door, and the door opened before anyone could react. A man in a fine and expensive suit walked in with authority. "Hartman, Parker."

Drake saw a familiar man who looked out of place. He assessed that the man was in his mid forties. He wore his salt-and-pepper gray hair short, side-parted, and meticulously styled. Drake thought his suit was a grade, maybe two, above standard police station uniform, even for a man in charge. He looked down from the man's blue eyes to the gold nameplate pinned to his suit coat where the pocket square might normally be. Drake read the nameplate: Police Chief John Peters.

Chief Peters walked up to the table and stood next to Drake. "So, you must be Mr. Drake."

Drake did not get up, but he extended a hand and shook hands with Chief Peters. "Chief."

"I received a call from downtown this morning," Chief Peters said. "I was told that I should be expecting you. Why don't we go to my office and have a word." He motioned toward the doorway.

Drake stood up.

To Hartman and Parker, Chief Peters said, "I'll have him back to you in few minutes. Give him access to anything he needs, and give him your full cooperation."

Parker and Hartman reacted with surprise and looked at each other.

Drake said, "Hartman, Detective Parker, why don't we have lunch. I'll buy. Noon?"

"Sure," Hartman said.

"Where?" Drake asked.

"How about the diner down the street, three blocks north on the west side?"

"Sure."

Chief Peters left the room, and Drake headed for the door.

As he exited the room, he heard Hartman say, "Interesting, very interesting."

He heard no comment from Detective Parker.

7

Drake followed the police chief into his office. He stood just inside the doorway and looked around at the pictures, awards, and citations that graced the walls. Drake had read about Chief Peters and his successes during his time on the force, which were detailed in a profile in the *Chicago Sun-Times* last year. Although Drake had known him personally now for just a few minutes, the success and confidence exhibited throughout the chief's office and in his demeanor were clear.

"Mr. Drake, please, have a seat," Chief Peters said as he walked around the desk.

Drake walked up to the desk, and they sat down across from each other.

Chief Peters stared at Drake then showed the slightest hint of a smile. Drake revealed nothing.

"It appears you have quite a bit of pull in this city, Mr. Drake."

"I didn't know."

"Is this a new line of work for you?"

"I'm just helping a friend."

"Right. Tell me something, Mr. Drake. Why does an

ex-journalist-turned-author get hired to investigate a cold murder case?"

Drake said nothing.

"Mr. Drake?"

"As chief, I assumed your office was downtown," Drake said, changing the topic.

Chief Peters seemed annoyed. "I do have an office downtown. But the 18th is my station, where I started, and so I keep an office here as well."

"Convenient," Drake said.

"So, let me ask again: why did *you* get hired to investigate a cold murder case?"

"Maybe because I have the skills to find a new angle."

"Or create one?"

Drake felt the jab—received the message—but did not react.

"I apologize," Chief Peters said. "That was uncalled for."

"I understand."

"That was my case, Mr. Drake."

"I know. You found the hand and were the lead investigator on the case. It appears you were quite thorough in your investigation, even going so far as to put quite a bit of pressure on the Mitchell family. That approach didn't go over well."

"That's an understatement. That family almost ended my career."

"But you carried on," Drake said, "and ultimately they were all cleared of any implication or wrongdoing."

"They were."

"Do they all still despise you?"

"All except Senator Mitchell," Chief Peters said. "He was

the only one who was fully cooperative, who understood the process, my responsibility."

"He's a politician."

"Sure, but . . . I don't know. He didn't have a problem with the investigation, ever. Actually, neither did Mrs. Mitchell. They just wanted to find their daughter's killer, finally put Sarah to rest, and end the nightmare."

"I understand," Drake said.

"So, what's your plan?"

"I'll review the case file, talk to a few people, and write up my report."

"That's it?" Chief Peters was not convinced.

"My employer just wants to put the issue to rest, once and for all."

"And who is your employer?"

"I'd rather not say."

The chief folded his hands, rested them on the desk in front of him, and leaned forward. "And you'll be able to do that for him—put it to rest?"

"Or her," Drake said. "It shouldn't take too long, maybe a week . . . or two."

Chief Peters considered Drake's response. He sat back in his chair. "All right then," he said, staring at Drake.

"All right then."

They glared at each other—quiet, unmoving, assessing. A chess game in progress.

Drake felt he had the better handle on the situation, and he relaxed. "Is there anything else?"

"You probably think I have a problem with you digging up this old case, my old case."

"I would understand if you did," Drake said, "and would be concerned if you didn't."

"Well, I don't. There is no one in this city who would like that murderer found and brought to justice more than me. That's why I will fully support and cooperate with your investigation."

"Thank you."

"If you, if we, can solve this case, it is likely that both of our careers will benefit from such an outcome. Wouldn't you agree, Mr. Drake?"

"It's just a job."

Now agitated, Chief Peters leaned forward again, his hands palm-down on the desk. "And that's what worries me. The last thing I need is for some supposed hotshot—someone who I don't know, and frankly, who I have no reason to trust—to come into my city and stir things up, only to leave me with all the mess to clean up."

Drake listened but did not respond.

"And I don't need the publicity."

"Unless you can finally bring the murderer to justice," Drake said.

Chief Peters settled back in his chair. "Mr. Drake. I do know of your past life as a journalist at the *Tribune,* the one newspaper in this city I read religiously and that seems to get it right a majority of the time. After I received the call this morning about your expected visit, I did some research, read some of your old articles, and your name came back to me. You were good, seemed you could always get the real story, no matter what it took or how many people you alienated. And you did alienate quite a few people."

"I suppose I did."

"And for some reason your new employer feels you have the experience, the ability, to approach the case from a different angle. I don't get it."

Drake shrugged.

"All I ask is that you promise me you will not release any information regarding this case—absolutely nothing—to the press or the public without my approval. Can you grant me that one consideration?"

"I can."

"All right then. Like I said, you and your employer have my support and the full support of my team. I will let everyone know to give you their complete cooperation."

"Thank you." Drake stood. "By the way, who called you to let you know that I was coming?"

"I'd rather not say."

"Of course." Drake reached across the desk and shook hands with Chief Peters. He walked toward the door then stopped and turned around. "Chief, is that your Mercedes out front?"

"It is."

"That's a very nice, expensive car," Drake said, and he walked out of the office and down the hall.

As Drake walked, he envisioned Chief Peters, standing firm with his arms folded across his chest and his eyes glaring, attempting to burn holes in Drake's back.

* * *

A little after noon, Drake, Hartman, and Parker met at City Diner, a breakfast and burger joint down the street a few blocks north of the station. They sat at a square table in the front corner of the establishment with a view of the street. The diner was not a place for a confidential discussion, as it was a popular lunch spot, especially for cops. Most of the other tables and stools at the counter were filled, and the noise level was rising. The waitress had already stopped by and had taken their orders.

"How's everything with the chief?" Hartman asked.

"Fine," Drake said.

"I still can't believe you're here, snooping around on a murder case."

"It shouldn't take long, maybe a couple of days."

Parker asked, "How can we help?"

"Like I told the chief, I'll just need to review the case file, talk to a few people, and write up my report."

"We've put in a request for all the physical evidence and case documents," Hartman said. "It's coming from Central Storage. Everything should arrive tomorrow morning."

"Good. I'll stop by for another visit tomorrow, maybe late morning, if that's all right with you."

"You'll have access to all of the online case documentation as well," Parker said. "I can help you with that."

"Thank you."

Drake looked at Parker, and their eyes locked momentarily, just like when they first met in the station conference room. Through his peripheral vision, he saw Hartman watching.

Drake broke the lock and turned to Hartman. "Mike, you were involved in the original investigation. Was there anything you found unusual? Anything you feel I should pay particular attention to?"

"It was a long time ago," Hartman said.

The waitress arrived with a full tray and set down a plate in front of each of them: corned beef for Hartman, pastrami for Drake, and tuna salad for Parker.

Drake took a bite of his sandwich then looked up at Hartman. He chewed and waited, expecting and wanting more. "You were saying."

Hartman took a bite of pickle, thought about Drake's question again, and appeared as though he was trying to remember. "I guess what was most unusual is that there wasn't much to go on. I was on a patrol that scoured that area for days, trying to find anyone who might have seen or heard anything. It was a total bust. We interviewed the conservatory staff and every shift of the zoo staff. Given the time of day, there weren't many people around. We even interviewed every tenant of every apartment building with a view of the park area."

"What about the family?" Drake asked.

"They're one of the most respected families in the state— hell, in the country."

"And?"

"The chief, he was the lead detective at the time, and he worked the family hard—some say too hard—and almost lost his job as a result."

"I heard that," Drake said. "Do you know the senator's son?"

"I do."

"Personally?"

"No," Hartman said. "Let's just say I've had the opportunity to meet him more times than I care to admit. He's a real piece of work."

"He's a son of a bitch," Parker said.

"Is that so?" Drake asked.

"I was on a security detail a couple of years ago, back when Jack Jr. was first running for an alderman seat. He was campaigning hard in the city, holding rallies, and getting everyone riled up. I met him. He has loose hands and thinks he's God's gift to women."

"Not your type?"

"He's a turd in a two thousand dollar suit," Parker said, "with a silver spoon still stuck in his mouth. Harvard educated—how, I'll never understand—and street stupid."

"It seems he left quite an impression." Drake turned to Hartman. "He was cleared?"

"He was . . . clean," Hartman said. "Spotless, with an airtight alibi. Almost too airtight."

"I read the crime scene report," Drake said, changing the topic.

"Really? We didn't give it to you yet."

"I'm resourceful."

"Sure you are." Hartman looked at Parker, who shrugged. To Drake he said, "And what did you figure out, from the report?"

"Just that the hand was left in the park, as if it was on display. No other physical evidence was found. The body was likely dumped."

"That's right," Hartman said.

"The murderer was making a statement with the hand, like it was personal," Drake said.

Hartman said, "The medical examiner's report noted that the hand was cleanly removed, postmortem and with precision instruments, carefully planned and executed. It was no irrational butcher job."

"Like I said, personal."

There was a moment of silence, then Drake stood up from the table. "I hate to eat and run, but I have an appointment."

"You didn't eat," Parker said.

"Help yourself." Drake pulled a wad of bills from his pocket, peeled off two twenties, and laid them on the table. "Mike, Detective Parker, thanks for your time."

"Wow, big spender," Hartman said.

Drake headed for the door.

"So, you'll grace us with your presence again tomorrow?" Hartman shouted.

Drake turned and waved. He opened the door and left the diner.

8

Drake was at The Book Loft early the next morning. For the second day in a row, he did not have a hangover. He was working in the back office of the store, which looked more like a storage room, crowded with boxed and loose books. He sat at a large wooden desk, reviewing some notes he had compiled. Faint light penetrated through the front windows of the store and into the office. A cigarette smoldered in the ashtray, creating a haze like a fog that had rolled in off the lake.

The night before in his apartment, Drake had done some research. There, at his desk and in front of his computer, he had spent a few hours digging through news articles from the *Chicago Tribune* archives. To his benefit, their network and computer security protocols were lax, and he had full, unrestricted access to everything the paper had ever printed, along with corresponding background and research materials, and even some articles that never made it to press. He also still had a few friends at the *Tribune*, and getting help to access the data he needed was not a challenge. The portfolio of documentation Thomas Engel had given him was elaborate and detailed, but Drake was not satisfied. Moreover, as Engel had alluded to, there were gaps that needed filling, dots that needed connecting. He had not identified anything new, but he did have a few drinks and had smoked heavier than usual while he worked, so while he was not hungover, he was a bit lethargic and had a scratchy throat.

He opened up the portfolio and set out again to digest its contents. He leafed through the pages as he had done before but stopped at the crime scene detail, the specific notes relating to Sarah Mitchell's hand that Peters had included in his report:

> Visually inspected the hand and the ground under and around it. The ground: brown-yellow grass covered with leaves—maple and of various colors—all moist from the morning dew. The hand: female, age undetermined but possibly fifteen to twenty-five, a left hand, dainty but with slender fingers, a substantial color difference notable between the darker shade of blue under the fingernails and the paler blue shade of the skin, and the skin was dry—completely dry. The ring: loosely fit on her pinky finger.

Her, Drake noted. Detective Peters had made it personal from the start.

> The ring band: silver in color but given the luster, more likely platinum. The opal: expensive and substantial at approximately three carats, encircled by twelve small but seemingly perfect diamonds. The wrist: fully intact and no watch present, the amputation cut encrusted with

blood, made approximately two inches up the forearm from the wrist joint. The cut: unhurried and likely made with a precision instrument, as evidenced by the clean edge of the flesh and the smooth cross-section surface of the forearm bones. Did not disrupt the scene and waited for the investigators and medical examiner to arrive.

Drake made some additional notes then reclined in his chair and pondered what he had read, his predicament.

He felt the need to go out, realized he could not afford to wait for the files and evidence to come from Central Storage.

Engel had not given him a deadline, and after ten years, there wasn't a need to rush the investigation now. The five grand a week with expenses could likely continue for as long as Drake wanted, but something nagged at him, twisted his gut, and made him feel uneasy about the state of the case. After reading everything that Engel had provided and all he could get his hands on at the *Tribune*, he could not understand how the case was ever closed. *What about the girl?* He could not understand how anyone could close the door on her, the severed hand and unrecovered body, a young woman in her prime, her life cut short and left to rot in a storage facility of buried cold cases.

And he wasn't comfortable with Engel's suggested approach to investigating the case. Drake felt there were even more holes than Engel had suggested.

His jacket hung on the back of his chair. He reached back and into the front right pocket and pulled out the Walther pistol he took from Ray Parsons. He pulled back the slide to inspect the chamber, to ensure once again that it was empty, and released it back. Satisfied, he put the gun back into his jacket pocket.

"Hey, Rita!"

Seconds later, Rita appeared in the doorway. "Yeah?"

"Can you get by without me here today?"

"You just got here."

"This research project . . . It's a little more work than I expected."

"You're not used to it," she said.

"What?"

"Work."

"You're funny."

"I'll be fine," she said. "Even when you're here, you're not really here."

Drake said nothing, and now he was reluctant to leave.

"Go on," she said. "Get out of here. I'll take care of the shop."

Drake thought about it for a moment then stood up from the desk and headed for the door. As he walked by her, he said, "Thanks. You're the best."

"I know. That's why you pay me so much."

"That's right," he said then left the shop.

* * *

Drake took a taxi to the far southwest side of the city, to an unincorporated area populated by gentleman's clubs, pawnshops, and strip malls, the types of enterprises shunned by most municipalities, along with single-level industrial buildings that housed light manufacturing businesses. The taxi approached a decrepit strip mall stretched out over two blocks that had more than a dozen businesses. All of the establishments looked the same, differing only by the neon signs mounted to the faded yellow brick above the glass windows and doorways.

At the end of the block, the taxi driver pulled into a parking lot, headed to the back, and stopped in front of a building that posted no signage. The building was low and wide, constructed of dirty, red brick. The roof was flat, and there were no windows. The brick facade was disrupted only by a single glass door, which was fitted on the inside with steel bars. Drake paid the driver, stepped out onto the sidewalk, and glanced left and right. He was not uncomfortable with the location or the sight of two punks smoking a joint at the corner of the building. He entered the building, and the taxi sped away.

A door buzzer announced his entrance.

Drake listened, heard nothing, then walked into and scanned the large, square room, the walls lined on three sides with glass display cases filled with handguns. Rifles and shotguns filled racks on the walls. To his right was a doorway, above which was a sign that read: SHOOTING RANGE.

A man came through the door at the back of the shop and stood behind the display case. He was an imposing, muscled man who stood six-foot-three and was a good two hundred and eighty pounds. He had a shaved head, a dark Van Dyke beard, and was not the kind of person to meet in a dark alley. However, Drake knew better. The man's name was Scotty, and he was Drake's oldest and best friend. Drake knew him to be a big teddy bear but with a killer instinct, friendly but dangerous just the same.

"Well, if you're not a sight for sore eyes," Scotty said. He spoke softly for such a big man, was polite, and possessed a voice of calm and reason.

Drake walked across the room. He approached Scotty and reached across the counter to shake hands with him.

"Drake, it's been a long time."

"It's good to see you."

"It's good to see you too. I was beginning to think we weren't friends anymore."

"Sorry, I've been busy."

"The life of a struggling novelist. How's the new book coming along?"

"It's not, but I finished the title page."

"Congratulations."

"And now I'm distracted," Drake said.

"Why is that?"

"You know of a guy by the name of Thomas Engel?"

"Can't say that I do."

Drake was not surprised. "Can you do a background check on him for me?"

"Of course."

"He showed up at my apartment the other day and offered me a job."

"Really."

"Wants me to look into a murder case: the Sarah Mitchell murder, ten years ago."

"The senator's daughter," Scotty said. "I remember. Her severed hand was left in the park by the conservatory."

"That's the one."

"That was a long time ago. The case is still open?"

"Went cold eight years ago."

"Why does this Mr. Engel care?"

Drake said, "Sarah Mitchell was his younger brother's fiancée. She was murdered while his brother was away. He was a Marine, killed in action. Engel made a promise to his brother to take care of her while he was away. He didn't keep his promise. He feels he needs to close the case once and for all, for his brother."

"Why you?"

"He thinks I can help."

"No, *why you*?" Scotty asked. "What does he know?"

"He seems to know quite a bit. That's why I need you to do a background on him."

Scotty looked at Drake with an expression of concern.

"Relax," Drake said. "Do the background, and let's see if we can find out what he knows."

"Will do."

Drake reached into his pocket. "I have a present for you." He pulled out Ray Parsons' Walther and laid it down on the glass.

Scotty picked up the gun, ejected the magazine, and inspected the chamber. "And where did you get this?" He raised the gun, lined it up with a point on the opposite wall, and nodded his approval.

"An old acquaintance, a guy I used to go to school with, asked me to hold it for him."

"Sure he did."

"And now it's yours," Drake said.

Scotty shrugged and put the gun in the display case in front of him. "Thanks. Have time for a shoot?"

"Why not."

"Trying something new today, or shall I get your old standby?"

"I don't like new."

Scotty nodded and disappeared through the door behind him.

Drake waited, looking around. It had been a while since his last visit, but the shop was the same. Scotty was the same. He took comfort in that realization. He didn't like new and didn't much care for change.

A moment later, Scotty came back through the door, holding a dark, wood box in both hands. He set the box down on the counter and lifted the lid so Drake could see the contents. Inside the box was another Walther pistol, this one a PP Model in pristine condition: .32-caliber, accommodated eight rounds in the magazine and one in the chamber, nickel plated, and handsomely engraved. Next to the pistol were three, nickel-plated magazines. Scotty turned around to the back wall and pulled a box of ammunition from the shelf.

Drake looked down at the gun, saw his other old friend. "I appreciate you taking care of it for me."

"My pleasure," Scotty said, closing the lid and picking up the box. He walked toward the shooting range door. "Shall we?"

"I'm right behind you."

9

Inside the shooting range, there were eight partitioned lanes. Drake and Scotty walked up to station four, and Scotty flipped a switch that illuminated the lane. He set the box down on the counter, opened it, and backed up. Drake stepped forward and took his place as he removed his jacket, which he hung on a hook on the left partition wall. He removed the gun and one of the magazines from the box, and the feeling of the cold steel in his hands created a sense of warmth in his chest. He loaded eight rounds, inserted the magazine into the butt of the pistol, and pulled back and released the slide, which loaded a round and armed the gun. He set the gun down and looked at Scotty.

"Target's at twenty-five feet," Scotty said. "Want me to move it up for you? It's been a long time."

Drake reached for the target control knob, which was mounted to a small box next to him. He turned and held the knob and watched as the target moved farther away.

"Seventy-five feet," Scotty said. "You're pretty sure of yourself."

From the counter in front of him, Drake picked up and put on the requisite eye and ear protection, then he picked up the gun. He raised the gun, and with a two-handed grip and staggered stance, he methodically fired eight shots in an even, timed manner. He lowered the gun, stared at the target, and set the gun down. He reached for the control knob and turned it in the opposite direction to bring the target back.

Scotty stepped up alongside Drake as the target arrived. "I guess it hasn't been that long."

Drake released the control knob and the target stopped three feet in front of them. The black center of the target was gone.

"Remember the first time you fired that gun?"

"I do."

Scotty was referring to their firearms field training at the Federal Law Enforcement Training Center in Glynco, Georgia. Wanting to make a good impression and, normal for him then, erring on the side of being overdressed, Drake had shown up in a suit. No one had told him about the casual dress code expected for training. Within the first thirty minutes of his arrival, a couple of the other trainees started razzing him, calling him James Bond and Gin-Boy, and they wouldn't let up. The men were FBI agents, experienced, back for an annual refresher course, and they took the opportunity to give the rookie a hard time. The rest of the class joined in and had fun with it, and Drake was tagged as a suck-up.

When the training class began, Officer Tyler Bridges, a retired Navy Seal member and the course instructor, unholstered his prized Walther to show the group. He acted as though he slept with the gun and never let it out of his sight. He didn't know that Drake, or anyone else in the group, could shoot at an expert level, so he thought he would single out the fancy boy and put the pressure on Drake with an easy bet. Bridges was so confident in his shooting skills, he offered up his gun as the prize. Bridges shot first, displaying mechanical precision and producing a tight grouping. Then it was Drake's turn. As Drake stepped forward, in his custom-fitted suit, he could still hear the old guys whispering and snickering. He loaded a fresh magazine into the instructor's gun, lined up his shot the same way he had done so many times before, let his breath out slowly before holding it just a second, and then emptied the magazine. After the sound repercussions from the shots faded, only silence remained. He beat the instructor's score and took ownership of his gun. The comments, whispering, and snickering had ceased, never to return for the remainder of the sessions.

"It was like taking candy from a baby," Drake said.

"I don't think Bridges ever recovered. Remember he said that gun was a prize he had brought home from active duty, from an Iraqi general his squad had taken down."

"I remember. And from the first time I shot it, I knew I'd never need another gun."

"It seems to work for you," Scotty said.

Drake reached into his pants pocket and pulled out a round of ammunition. He held it up between two fingers for Scotty to look at.

Scotty inspected it. "Hmm. You still have some?"

"Engel gave it to me," Drake said.

"Where did *he* get it?"

"I don't know. I thought you had the only remaining supply."

"I do," Scotty said, "locked in a safe in the back. Only I have the combination, and the fingerprints, to get at them."

"Exactly."

"I'll look into it," Scotty said, perplexed.

"I'd appreciate it." Drake picked up the gun. "Mind if I take this?"

"For your writing?"

"Funny."

"It's yours. Need a holster?"

"I still have my old shoulder harness," Drake said, "stuffed in a box somewhere." He stuck the gun in his back waistband then grabbed the other magazines from the box and put them in his front pocket. He took his jacket from the hook and put it on.

"Be careful," Scotty said. "You don't have a permit to carry any more."

"I'll check back with you, in a day or so. If you find out anything, call me."

"Will do."

Drake walked toward the door.

Scotty let him get a few steps away. "Drake?"

Drake turned around. "Yeah?"

"It's good to see you."

"You too," Drake said, and he left the range.

* * *

The Walther PP pistol, while classic in its styling and with a design that has proven the test of time, was not without its troubles, especially since the days when the manufacturing of the gun left Germany and came to the United States.

Fortunately, Drake's gun was produced as a custom piece in the Walther factory in Ulm, Germany, and from the time he took possession, it rarely had mechanical issues. After just a short time, the gun became a part of Drake, part of who he was and what he could be, and he began to understand how the Iraqi general and Officer Bridges must have felt when they owned it.

The gun's sporadic problem with feeding a cartridge into the chamber after firing didn't matter much to Drake. If he wanted to, which he didn't, he could tell you that he never needed the second round in the magazine; the one in the chamber was sufficient. His friend Scotty knew he needed only one shot, as did the few remaining people who knew him from the Agency. Others could ask Drake, but he wouldn't tell them. Those who pressed him in a confrontation would find out the hard way.

He had not been to the range for quite some time, but shooting a gun was like riding a bike. Back when he started working at the Agency, he began a routine of going to the range, and he went often, working up to shooting a thousand rounds at each session. At the time, his approach to shooting a pistol was simple: draw the gun from his holster, aim, fire one shot, and return the gun to the holster. Each time he went to the range, he practiced diligently to perfect that same sequence of moves, a thousand times over. His shooting technique was so practiced and proficient that it became instinctual and automatic. He knew exactly where the gun rested in its shoulder holster, where his hand would hit the butt of the gun, and the amount of force required to pull it from the holster and get it to the resting position in front of him. Then, when prompted and in the matter of a second, he would have the gun leveled, aimed, finger on the trigger, and ready to shoot when forced to do so.

No one told him to pursue such a regimen of shooting. No one at the Agency ever suggested it. His primary responsibility, his job, was to test ammunition, rounds designed by the Agency that he would likely never see or use outside of the range. He tested the ammunition thoroughly, took his job seriously. They hoped to get a hundred, maybe two hundred rounds tested each time he showed up at the range, and Drake kept asking for more. The Agency didn't care. Their program was funded indefinitely, and they figured the more the ammunition was tested, the better the data for use in future product development.

Initially, shooting the additional rounds took a toll on Drake's body, but after a few weeks, the aches and pains subsided and his strength and resilience increased, as did his overall skill and accuracy. The data was beneficial for Drake as well. Sure, he perfected his shot, but he also learned early on that he could rely on certain types of ammunition while others were best left on the design table.

10

Drake approached the Sarah Mitchell crime scene from a distance. It had been ten years, and he wondered if the conservatory location, the park, was different now. He wanted to retrace Peters' steps, as detailed in the police report Engel had provided, so Drake had started in the parking lot alongside the conservatory building and walked around toward the front entrance. Peters had tried the doors and found them locked. The doors were open now, a trickle of people entering and leaving the building. Drake proceeded east across an expanse of grass, as Peters had, toward a thick stand of trees bordering the property. He walked with calculated and careful steps as he crossed the park, hoping a piece of the puzzle might come to him, something Peters and everyone else might have missed, so he could finish the job and get back to his writing. He appreciated having the work and the cash, but he needed and wanted answers—about who killed Sarah Mitchell and why—to put Sarah and the case to rest, and so he could be done with it all. He observed the dying but still manicured grass and the flowerbeds that formed the perimeter of the park. There were a few people walking the grounds, and there was a young couple seated on a park bench enjoy-ing their lunch. Everything appeared normal to Drake, as he expected.

As he approached the site where the suspected murderer had left the hand ten years ago, he stopped and looked around. He observed the ground and the surrounding area. He looked up at the long iron fence that bordered the park. He listened to the blowing wind and the songs of the few birds that lin-gered in nearby trees. He breathed in the cool autumn air and enjoyed the peaceful solitude.

"This is quite a day, Mr. Drake."

Drake turned around.

Chief Peters walked toward him.

"Hey, Chief. Thanks for agreeing to meet me."

"I guess I should thank you for the courtesy call. Frankly, I didn't expect to hear from you, didn't expect to hear about your investigation, until you crossed someone and I got the call from the brass above telling me to get you in line."

"It was your case," Drake said. "It's still your case."

Chief Peters nodded. "So, what's on your mind?"

"I guess the simple question is, how could you have closed the case?"

Chief Peters thought about the question, his hands in the front pockets of his dark gabardine trench coat, and he looked around to see who was close. "Sometimes, you just have to let it go."

"I don't believe that."

They stared at each other.

"I'm sorry about your daughter," Drake said.

Chief Peters didn't flinch.

"I read about the accident," Drake said. "It was terrible. I have two daughters of my own and can't even imagine what I'd do if anything happened to either of them."

"Yeah."

Drake looked up at the clear sky. "The accident happened around the time of the Sarah Mitchell murder."

"Three months before. It was a tough time for us . . . my wife was crushed." He paused and seemed to grit his teeth. "I had just gone back to work the week earlier, was trying to get back into the routine, and then I received the call about the hand. It was brutal. Not a way to start a day. From the moment I saw it, the hand, the case became personal." He stared at the ground.

"I remember like it was just yesterday: walking up near to the hand and feeling it somehow motioning for me to come closer, kneeling down on the grass, and studying it. I was mesmerized. In my fifteen years on the police force, I'd seen my fair share of crime scenes but nothing quite like that one. The sight of a severed hand was grisly and morbid, but my immediate reaction—tasting burning and sour bile in the back of my throat—surprised me. It was cold outside, but I was sweating, and I remember feeling a knot growing in my stomach as I tried to imagine the young woman who once owned the hand—a young, beautiful, and vibrant woman, a daughter of a man and woman who would surely be tortured by the gruesome memory for the rest of their lives. I remember the anger I felt."

He continued to stare at the ground, seemed lost in the memory. He looked up at Drake.

Drake said nothing.

Chief Peters said, "Another family had lost a daughter, senselessly, and I wasn't going to stop until I found out what had happened, until I brought that maniac to justice. That sick son of a bitch. It's why I pushed so hard, on everyone, for two years of my life."

"But then you let it go."

"Yeah, I did." Chief Peters closed his eyes, seemed to be taking himself back in time, trying to remember, or maybe forget. The muscles in his jaw tightened.

Drake remained quiet, watched him, and waited.

"Every day, I thought about Sarah Mitchell. She was only eighteen, for Christ's sake. She was a beautiful young woman, an accomplished musician, kind, gentle . . . She was just a little girl." He paused. "And every day, I thought of my daughter . . . just a little girl." He choked up.

"I think I understand," Drake said.

"I doubt it. For those two years, I was obsessed with the case. I was possessed by the case, by the sight of the hand. It haunted me. I'd have this recurring nightmare, of my daughter, stuck in that car, unable to get out, waving at me to help her . . . with Sarah Mitchell's hand." He paused again, looked around.

"So you let it go. It's understandable."

"The case was dead and I had to, not only for personal reasons, so I could move on, but so that other people could move on as well. The family was cleared, every lead—the few we had—had been fully investigated, every possibility explored, and I was getting pressure from the chief at the time, who was getting his balls busted by the mayor. The chief told me to close the case, a recommendation he made strongly, urging the necessity of my prompt action if I ever wanted to be promoted. So the case was closed."

Drake didn't know what to say, so he fell back on what was still on his mind. "Again, I'm sorry about your daughter."

"I appreciate that."

Drake heard a faint squeak of metal on metal, and he turned back toward the conservatory building, which stood like a scowling, cold, dark statue. Chief Peters looked back as well. Drake scanned the metal-framed glass panels that formed the windows and roof of the building, the reflection of the high sun bouncing off the uniform and straight slope of the roof, interrupted only by the one open panel that was likely just opened by someone inside.

"It's funny," Chief Peters said.

"What is?"

"I heard that same sound, that squeak, the morning I was here at the crime scene . . . ten years ago."

"What was it?"

"I don't know. Didn't think anything of it."

"Was that noted in your report?"

Chief Peters ignored the question and looked back at the ground of the crime scene.

"Chief, is there anything else you can tell me?"

"We're not reopening this case, Mr. Drake."

Drake didn't say anything.

"Do we understand each other?"

"We do."

"All right then." Chief Peters walked away, made it only a few steps, and stopped. He turned back to Drake, and it seemed his demeanor had changed. "If you come up with anything, or if you have any more questions, please call me."

"I will. Thanks."

The chief walked across the park to his car at the street. Drake watched until the chief was back in his car and driving away.

Drake looked at the conservatory building. There were a few people going in through the front doors. He turned and looked up at the majestic towers of the Belden-Stratford.

He decided to pay the building a visit.

* * *

Drake met the building manager at the Belden-Stratford, a property that an investment company had recently converted from a hotel to luxury apartment rentals. The man did not welcome the unsolicited distraction and had no recollection whatsoever of the events that had transpired in the neighborhood ten years earlier. He was out of state and in college at the time. He didn't know of Senator Mitchell or the Mitchell family and expressed no interest in politics. Drake provided a brief summary of the case, and the manager became defensive. It was bad publicity at the time, and Drake assumed it was not the kind of information the manager wanted circulating around with his tenants, so he was not surprised when the man clammed up. Drake asked some more questions, pushed a little, but got nowhere.

Drake cut his interview short when Detective Parker called and told him that the case documentation had arrived and was waiting for him. He left the Belden-Stratford, flagged down a taxi, and headed back to the 18th District Police Station.

Drake entered the police station with little fanfare. He fully expected the watch commander—the same one he had met on his first visit—to make a comment about his name, but instead, the guy acted like he was expecting him and like Drake was an already accepted member of the force, which Drake thought was odd and unusual. And unwanted.

He realized that word from the top—good word—must have made its way around the station, which would make his life and job much easier. The watch commander directed him to a quiet conference room on the rear side of the building, where Drake sat at a large table and went to work reviewing the boxes of case documents. He also had Engel's portfolio with him, and as he reviewed each new document, he checked off the document name and number on the provided inventory list then reviewed the noted information and compared those details to the information from Engel, looking for gaps or discrepancies.

On the table was a laptop computer, police-issued. He turned on the machine and signed on using the system credentials the watch commander had given him. He accessed case records and related documents, some that were duplicates of what he found in the box, but he focused on the "online storage only" category. Contrary to what he had said to Engel, Drake was very much a computer guy, but even so, the police records system was rudimentary, intuitive, and easy to navigate. He entered several queries, read and analyzed the information returned, and made some notes in his portfolio.

A knock on the door broke the silence and splintered his concentration.

"Come in," Drake said.

The door opened, and Detective Parker walked in. "Hi. Just thought I'd check in—to see if you need anything."

He was surprised that he wasn't annoyed at the interruption. "I'm fine, thanks."

"How long have you been at it?"

"Long enough to know I don't envy your job."

"Anything yet?"

"No."

He looked at her. She looked at him. Drake turned toward the computer and entered his next query, another document search. He wasn't trying to be rude and hoped it didn't come across that way; he just had work to do.

She watched him for a bit then realized that no further conversation was likely. "Well, I'll leave you to it then."

Drake didn't respond; he was focused on the report displayed on the screen.

"I'm just down the hall if you need anything."

"Thanks," Drake said. He looked at her.

She acknowledged his response with a nod. It seemed she was not surprised by his standoffish demeanor and did not appear offended. That was good. However, when she left the room, she slammed the door closed behind her.

"Hmm." Drake turned to the computer and went back to work.

* * *

Drake spent the better part of the day at the police station. While not gratifying in any way, going through the case documentation was a necessary task to get a full understanding of how the case had progressed from the onset and the details that led up to the decision to close it, unsolved. It was also necessary so he could gauge the totality and quality of Engel's information. It was clear to Drake that Engel had been a busy man for many years and had effectively researched every available detail of the case. Through his analysis, Engel had found quite a few gaps in consistency as well as some significant holes in the reports from the involved personnel. It was not clear to Drake if the police had handled the case poorly or if it was a deficiency in the reporting and documentation methods at the time. Either way, he was glad he had Engel's information as it provided a more complete and objective perspective.

Drake left the 18th District Police Station just before seven and stopped for a quick dinner at the diner down the street. It was less crowded this time, and he took a stool at the counter, ordered, and tried to read the newspaper left by a previous customer. Along with his sandwich—roast beef this time—he also had coffee, which wasn't quite satisfying since it was again black and without a kick, so on the way home, he stopped for a drink at Jameson's, a local bar down the street from the diner. It was where all the cops congregated to drink and sedate the troubles of the day. But really, he wanted to talk with Detective Parker. She had called him just as he was leaving the station—said she wanted to share something she had learned about the case.

When he arrived at the bar, Drake took the only open booth in the back. He ordered a glass of bourbon, neat, and when it arrived, he downed it and ordered another while the waitress was still there. Now, he sat in the dimly lit, quiet booth and sorted through the facts of the case in his mind, wondering what Detective Parker might have uncovered.

He knew the exact moment when she walked into the bar. There were many welcoming shouts and a few inappropriate comments—the stuff of back lots and locker rooms. She saw Drake, cut through the crowd to the back of the room, and approached his booth.

"Good evening," Drake said.

"I'm glad I caught you earlier and that you could meet me right away."

"It's either this or I go home and play with my cat."

"You have a cat?" she asked.

"No."

Parker thought for a second about their quick exchange and shrugged it off. She stood by the booth facing Drake, waiting. She looked the same as she did the day before, but the color of her suit was gray and her blouse was white.

Drake said, "Please, have a seat."

Parker slid in, felt the cracked leather of the seat, and glanced at Drake's drink. She looked up into his eyes.

"That's quite a welcoming party out there. Regulars from the 18th?"

"Mostly," she said. "It's a good group. I don't come here too often, which is why I get a few reactions and comments when I come in. It's inappropriate, I know, but they're harmless."

"They know a good thing when they see it."

"Yeah, sure."

The waitress approached their table. She seemed too old to be working in such an establishment and appeared tired, but she still made the effort to smile. To Parker, she said, "Hi, hon, what can I get for you?"

"I'll have a beer. Whatever you have on tap."

"Heineken okay?"

"That'll be fine."

The waitress looked at Drake's glass. "Drake, another?"

"Please."

The waitress hurried away. Drake folded his hands around his drink and stared at Parker.

"Drake, huh? Hartman told me to call you Sebastian. Said you'd prefer it."

He smirked. "Drake is fine."

"Have you been here before?"

"First time."

"And on a first-name basis with the waitress. It's like you're a regular here already."

"She asked my name. I told her."

They looked at each other for a long moment, remained quiet. He was feeling her out, wondering what she was thinking, and felt she was doing the same. There was an obvious mutual attraction, Drake thought, and he didn't feel it was necessary to rush and end the silence or the captivation.

Drake said, "So, you want to talk about the case?"

"Even though the chief has given his full support to your review of the case, I'm not supposed to spend time on it."

"Why's that?"

"Hartman and I have a full case load. Plus, the chief gave a direct order. He doesn't think your efforts will amount to anything."

"Interesting."

"After we met yesterday, I looked at some of the filed reports, those available online. Let's just say I got hooked. I can't believe the case was never solved, that some maniac killer is still out there, somewhere, maybe capable of doing it again. Plus, that poor girl—to cut off her hand—that's just sick. Who would do something like that?"

Drake said nothing, understood how she felt.

"Do you know she was a piano prodigy?" Parker asked.

"I do."

"You've reviewed the interview list?"

"I have," Drake said.

"Anything you want to talk about?"

"Not really."

The waitress arrived with the drinks. She set them down and took Drake's empty glass.

"Thank you," Parker said.

"Thank you," Drake added.

The waitress winked at Drake and left. Drake and Parker stared at each other again, and it was clear to Drake that they were each trying to figure out the other's play, what the other person knew. She took a sip of beer. He swallowed down half of the contents of his glass.

Not willing to wait any longer, Parker said, "So, I've reviewed the interview list as well, last night, on my own time."

Drake was impressed with her diligence and defiance of authority.

She said, "A case like this, the murderer is usually some-one the victim knows: a family member, a friend, a lover, a want-to-be lover. Everyone in the Mitchell family was a primary suspect, but all were cleared, quickly. *Very quickly."* She thought about the last statement. "A political family like that, you'd think they'd have lots of enemies, probably still do, but nothing was uncovered. Sarah Mitchell disappeared just months before the senator's re-election, so there were some who believed that the opposing party had something to do with it. A one-week witch-hunt ensued then fizzled out. The housekeeping staff—zip. The fiancé—he was in another country. Friends, neighbors—again, there was nothing. And on top of all that, there were no witnesses, not a single one. I realized it happened during the night or early morning, but in a city like Chicago, how is it possible that a maniac—a psychopath—can not only murder a young woman, but leave her severed hand on display in a park and not be seen, by anyone?"

It was obvious to Drake that she was uncomfortable with the circumstances. "You've been busy."

"You're right."

"So, what's on your mind?"

"There was nothing enlightening in the online files," she said, "so when the boxes came over from Central today, I looked through them. And I think I found something."

"What?"

"Billy Taylor."

Drake stared, remained quiet.

She said, "Know the name?"

"I do."

"Billy Taylor," she said again. "Neighborhood kid. Had known Sarah Mitchell for a long time. During the investigation, he came forward, offering to help. Said he knew her better than anyone, that they were *close.*"

"What do you think, romantically?" Drake asked.

She shrugged. "Maybe in *his* mind. He was younger and, it seems he might be a little slow. The report said he had a learning disability but nothing more specific. It seems he was a good kid, but not up to the Mitchell family standards, I suspect. Billy was not ever going to be recruited by the University of Chicago or become some east coast Harvard boy. For some reason, though, Sarah seemed to always go out of her way to befriend him, keep an eye on him, protect him. Since he offered to help, he was interviewed and let go."

"So?"

"Do you know who Billy Taylor's father was?"

"Yeah. Former Police Chief Cecil Taylor. Formerly alive as well. So?"

"So, I don't know. It's just a hunch . . ." She looked down at her beer, took a sip, and thought through the possibility.

"Tell me," Drake said.

She looked around, felt assured that no one could hear their conversation. "Chief Taylor was a close friend of Senator Mitchell. The interview notes are weak on the topic, which surprised me. Billy might have known something, but based on the filed report, the investigators just humored him with a few routine questions and then sent him on his way. Like the rest of the family, he was cleared, quickly."

"You think the chief made it go away, maybe minimized the relevance of what Billy knew?"

"He certainly could have."

Drake shook his head. "That's thin."

"You should talk to Billy," Parker said.

"I should?"

"He's close by, works at a grocery store in Bridgeport."

Drake downed his drink like a shot but said nothing.

"What would it hurt?" she asked. "Maybe he knows or remembers something."

"Maybe."

"So, you'll talk to him?"

"I'll think about it."

They sat and looked at each other, neither of them uncomfortable with their muted conversation. Drake didn't tell her that Engel had included a similar suggestion in *his* notes, that he had an even stronger inclination to suggest that Drake pursue the lead and talk with Billy Taylor—to find out what he really wanted to say back at the time of the incident. Drake raised his empty glass and sucked fumes.

"Okay, well, thanks for your time," Parker said. She stood up from the table.

"I'll walk out with you," Drake said. He slid out of the booth and left money on the table to cover the tab.

Parker headed for the front door, and Drake followed close behind.

They stepped out onto the sidewalk. It was raining lightly, small drops and mist. She turned toward him. "Where are you parked?"

"I walked," he said.

"C'mon, I'll give you a ride."

"No, I'm not far."

"You'll get soaked."

"Really, I won't melt."

She pointed down the street. "I'm right over here. C'mon, I'll drive you. I'm not taking 'no' for an answer."

Drake looked up and down the street, assessed the distance to her car, looked up at the falling rain, and considered the offer. "Thanks."

They hurried over to Parker's car, jumped in, and drove away.

11

Detective Parker pulled her car over toward the curb and rolled it forward up the street. The rain had picked up in the few minutes since they left the bar, and it was enough to clear the street of other cars and any pedestrians. The wipers had a tough time keeping up, and there was a continuous drumbeat on the roof of the car. She strained to see through the wavy windshield and the side window as she searched for building numbers.

"Right here is good," Drake said.

Parker stopped the car, put the transmission into park, and turned off the engine. With both hands on the steering wheel and looking forward through the windshield she said, "Have time for another drink?"

Drake looked at her, his head cocked to one side. "Are you inviting yourself up?"

"I want to see your cat."

Drake smiled. "Why not."

They exited the car and hurried up to the entrance of Drake's building, dodging puddles along the way. He held the door open for her then followed her inside. He led her to the stairwell and up to the third floor. They exited the

stairwell into the dimly lit hallway and Drake led the way
to his apartment.

He pulled a ring of keys from his jacket, unlocked the
single deadbolt, and walked inside. He flicked a light switch
that illuminated the short hallway and switched on a floor
lamp in the living room. Parker followed and closed the door
behind her. Drake walked into the living room, took off his
jacket, and laid it on a chair.

Parker entered the room and looked around. "Nice place."

"Thank you." Drake could tell that she wasn't impressed.

"What's that smell?" she asked, crinkling her nose.

"The cleaning staff doesn't come until tomorrow."

"Do you smoke?"

"A little. Please, make yourself comfortable." He directed
her toward the weathered leather sofa by the bare windows.
She walked over, cleared away the mess of newspapers and
magazines, and sat down. She did not look comfortable.

Drake said, "I have bourbon . . . and water."

"Bourbon is fine."

He walked over to his desk and pulled a bottle and two
glasses from the bottom drawer. With his back to her, he
held the glasses up to the light to inspect them. Comfortable
that they were usable, he poured an inch of bourbon into
each glass then carried them over to the sofa. He handed
her a glass and sat in the club chair facing her.

"Cheers," she said, and they drank.

She looked around the large, quiet room. "So, this is the
way a writer lives."

"Yeah. It works for me."

"Why are you working on this case, when you're a writer?"

"I seem to be getting that question a lot." He took a gulp of his drink and stared at her.

She stared back. "So?"

"It's interesting."

"I see." She sighed and appeared to realize that talking to Drake was going to be an effort, but she was determined. "You have some past experience that makes you qualified for such a job?"

"You could say that."

"Are you working on a new book?"

"I am."

"What's it about?"

"I'm still trying to figure that out."

"Will it be out soon?"

Drake stood, walked over to the desk, and refilled his glass. He looked at her.

She said, "I have trouble staying focused to write up a police report. I don't know how you do it."

Drake took another gulp.

"I hope I get to read it some day . . . your book, that is."

Drake nodded, accepting her request as a possibility.

Parker was obviously frustrated with the conversation, and she let out another sigh. "Well, thanks for the drink. I should be going." She set her glass on the side table and stood up. She reached into her jacket, pulled out a business card, and set it down next to the glass. "If I can be of any help, on the case, feel free to call."

"Thanks."

"Okay. I'll let myself out," she said and walked toward the door.

As she reached for the doorknob, Drake stopped her. "Detective Parker."

She turned around.

He walked toward her. "Thanks for putting your time on this." He stood before her, close. "I appreciate it."

She blushed. "You're welcome."

Taking her time and never breaking her gaze, she moved closer. She opened her blazer and pressed her breasts into his chest as she looked up at him. He didn't move. She rose on her tiptoes and inhaled his scent as she brushed harder up against him and nestled her nose in the crook of his neck. She put her mouth up to his ear and made her best attempt at a purring sound, like a cat. She pulled back and looked into his eyes.

Drake lowered his head and kissed her, and her response was immediate. She wrapped her arms around his neck, tight, and pulled herself closer. They kissed passionately as their hands began to roam—touching, exploring—and their lips mashed together. While still kissing, Drake led her toward the bedroom, and together, they surrendered to the darkness.

* * *

The next morning, Drake woke up earlier than usual. His eyes had popped open, alert and without warning from an alarm, at six o'clock. Prompted and driven by an unrecognized force, he was in and out of the shower and at his desk by six-thirty, back at work on his novel. He was dressed for the day in jeans and a black T-shirt and felt refreshed and engaged in his work from the moment he sat down. He tapped away at the keyboard of his computer, all of his fingers in motion, with unbridled determination. A lit cigarette was in the ashtray on his desk, relatively untouched and smoldering. His coffee was getting cold.

He stared at the words on the screen.

> *Her hand was slender and beautiful, and it looked like it was made of fine porcelain. But it was cold and tinted blue and no longer attached to the rest of her body. The hand looked like it could be on display at an art museum, resting on its palm and fingertips, each of the fingers bent slightly to give view to the next. Still fitted on the curved pinky finger was a simple yet elegant opal and diamond ring. The sun was just coming up over the horizon on the eastern side of Lake Michigan, and the hand was set upon a thick bed of fire-orange and red maple leaves, still moist from the morning dew. The hand was dry. The crusted blood at the severed wrist seemed to blend into the leaves, creating the impression that it was sticking out from beneath, that maybe the owner of the hand was resting below the bed of leaves. She was not.*

The words had appeared on the page in a single burst of activity, the picture in his mind throwing off the words like a photograph exploding out of his head into a thousand little pieces—words—and then forming back together again as a single and clear vision on the page. He wasn't sure where the vision would end up in his story but knew he would find a place for it. He read the words again and thought of Sarah Mitchell.

He took a quick drag from his cigarette and set it back in the ashtray. He exhaled with a sense of urgency. He felt invigorated, a feeling of excitement in his chest like a quickened heartbeat, and it seemed he wasn't quite finished with his task. His fingers went back to work on the keyboard.

After an hour of uninterrupted work, he heard rustling then footsteps coming from the bedroom. His eyes remained fixed on the computer screen. The thoughts and the words were spilling out of him and onto the page, and he didn't dare stop.

"Come back to bed."

He turned his head and saw Angie standing in the doorway of the bedroom, wide-eyed and appearing energized. "Good morning," he said while still typing to finish the sentence.

"Come on, it's still early," she said, her voice sultry and hoarse from sleep.

He looked at the screen then back toward the bedroom.

She raised an arm up against the doorjamb and winked at him.

Damn. He liked what he saw. Her curly, black hair was perfect, tickled her bare shoulders, and it seemed her face was glowing. She was holding a bed sheet up to her chin, and he could see the faint outline of her naked body behind the sheet. A memory of the night before came to him.

"What are you doing?" she asked.

Drake lifted the coffee mug from his desk and sipped, gazing at her and recollecting the fresh vision. He set the cup down and took a drag from his cigarette. "Writing. I woke up with an idea, a burning idea. I need to get it down while it's fresh and memorable."

"Can it wait?" she asked, inching the sheet lower.

Don't. "If I wait, I may lose it . . . forever." He turned back to his computer and continued typing, engrossed again in his story, in the words. He could tell that she hadn't moved, so he glanced back.

She pouted, appeared she understood but was still disappointed, and went back into the bedroom.

Drake continued typing, the words appearing across the screen, word after word, line after line, in rapid succession and in a manner he had not experienced in some time. He snuck in a drag from his cigarette when he needed to look at his notes. He was on a roll, and he felt good about the progress he had made so far.

Minutes later, he again heard rustling in the bedroom and caught sight of Angie as she stepped into the bedroom doorway. She stopped there, this time fully dressed, and he watched as she tightened her belt and adjusted her gun holster as she gazed at him.

She's beautiful. He considered the possibility that she was even more attractive and intriguing with her clothes on. He lit a cigarette and smiled at her.

"What are you smiling at?"

He turned back toward his computer and continued typing.

"I have to go," she said and walked toward him. She stepped up behind him, and he could sense she was looking over his shoulder.

"Can I read what you've written?" she asked.

"When it's done," Drake said, his eyes glued to the page. He read the last line he had typed and mouthed the words.

She moved close alongside him, leaned down in front of his face, and planted a long, wet kiss on his lips. She straightened and walked toward the door.

"Angie," Drake said.

She turned around.

"When it's done."

"Okay. I look forward to it."

The phone on Drake's desk rang, and he answered the call. "Hello?"

"Drake, it's Scotty."

"Good morning."

Drake looked up at Angie. She realized their conversation was over and expressed disappointment.

Into the phone, Drake said, "One minute." To Angie, he said, "I'm sorry, I need to take this."

"Go ahead, I understand."

"You're sure?"

"Go on." She waved a hand and smiled. "I'll see you again."

"You will."

She turned, walked down the hallway, and let herself out.

Drake watched her as far as he could, waited to hear the door close, and returned his attention to the call. "Sorry, I'm back."

"Who was that?" Scotty asked.

"The cleaning lady."

"She works interesting hours. Anyway, I did the background on Engel. He's quite an interesting fellow."

"Interesting how?"

"He has an awful lot of resources available to him, that's for sure, not the least of which is a net worth of about $500 million. Funny thing is, there's no trace of how he accumulated all of his wealth. As of now, the majority of his assets sit in a charitable trust that he controls. It appears his objective is to give it all away."

"He told me he was a philanthropist," Drake said.

"It appears he was telling the truth. Seems he's done a lot of good for a lot of people."

"What else?"

"He has a lot of friends—very important and influential friends. Using Agency resources, I was able to ID his past business and personal affiliations over the last twenty years."

"He was being tracked?"

"It appears so," Scotty said.

"By the Agency?"

"Yeah. But I couldn't find any reason why. He wasn't CIA, FBI, or anything else. It's possible he was just important enough, or rich enough, to have been investigated."

"That's unusual," Drake said.

"Yeah. There's not much there. He's had contact with lots of CEOs, venture capitalists, socialites, a full Hollywood A-list, and even some religious leaders."

"Interesting. Anything else?"

"It's strange." Scotty paused. "It appears he's been cleansed."

"What?"

"All his current information, for the last twenty years, appears complete and accurate. His past, however, everything before then, is a blank slate. Nothing in the Agency archives or any public database. It's like he never existed until twenty years ago."

Drake remained silent.

"His past was swept away and buried," Scotty said. "Just like you."

"I was afraid you were going to say that."

"I'll keep digging, but in the meantime, be careful."

"I will. Thanks." Drake hung up the phone. He lit another cigarette and replayed the discussion he just had. *Just like you*. He stared at his computer, waited a minute, and started to type again.

12

Drake heard a knock at the door, and he looked up at the wall clock. It was one o'clock in the afternoon. He had been writing, unrestrained, since Scotty had called and was surprised when he realized how much time had lapsed. For five hours, he had typed and smoked, and with the exceptions of a few bathroom and coffee trips, he hadn't left his desk.

Over the years, Drake's writing creativity and productivity came and went, and he couldn't tell you what combination of variables caused the switch in his head to flip to "obsessed and productive." Years ago, when working on his first book, he was a disciplined and self-imposed taskmaster, always keeping to a strict schedule. By his third book, he was spending more time in his office and producing less, but he couldn't tell you why. Maybe the fire had burned out some. Smoking seemed to always be a constant and had no effect either way. Alcohol seemed to open up his creative thought process but only to a certain point. Excessive consumption just made him drunk and shut him down, threw him down into a hole he had difficulty getting out of. Stress seemed to shut him down as well, and he found it difficult to put himself into the heads of his characters when he couldn't get out of his own head.

The last few days were different, and the events of those days had turned things around for him, for his writing. He had been out of the apartment and into the world of real stories, had interacted with living and breathing people, and had become interested in the Sarah Mitchell case. The young, dead girl intrigued him but at the moment, he couldn't explain why. He had some money and a new book contract. He had cut back on his alcohol consumption. And he had met Ms. Angie Parker.

The knock sounded again, but Drake stayed put.

Whatever variables were in play right now, Drake wasn't going to overthink or question them. He had made more progress on his book in the last five hours than he had in the last five weeks, and he had to play the streak.

There was another knock, this time harder and more forceful.

"Sebastian?" It was a woman's voice on the opposite side of the door.

Drake knew who it was and did not reply.

"Sebastian? It's me, Karen, your favorite ex-wife."

Drake heard the fumbling of keys then a key being inserted into the door lock. He leaned over to peer down the hallway and watched as the deadbolt knob turned, followed by the turning of the doorknob below it.

He leaned back over and scribbled some thoughts on the notepad in front of him. *I need to get it down while it's fresh and memorable.*

The door swung open, and he looked back down the

hallway. His ex-wife, Karen Drake, was standing at the threshold. She stayed in the entryway for a moment, maybe expecting a welcome of some sort. When one didn't come, she walked down the hallway and into the room, leaving the door open.

Drake didn't care for the interruption, the break from his often elusive but now-focused writing streak, but he was somewhat glad to see her just the same. She looked as she did the last time he had seen her. She was tall and slender, naturally attractive with long, straight, dark brown hair. She smiled without effort, displaying straight teeth in a shade of white Drake could only wish for. Her clothes were different though. She wore tight jeans with cowboy boots, a look that Drake thought, while understated and casual, highlighted and even accentuated the key aspects of her lower anatomy, her legs in particular. Up top, she wore a loose, knit sweater, beige, that left much, but not everything, to the imagination. The other difference was that this time, she was holding a stack of mail.

Drake and Karen had been divorced for over a year now. She left him and took the house, the kids, and half of everything—half that she more than deserved and that Drake never questioned. She had always understood Drake's personal and career aspirations and needs, but only to an extent. She, like most people, had limits. He knew she would never say it to his face, but Drake felt she still had feelings for him, that she might even still love him. She just couldn't live with him anymore, that much he understood, what with the alienation and abandonment that came with his approach to writing. She was the only one who could call him "Sebastian," the only one who, as the mother of his children, he would allow such an unquestionable and irrevocable right. She was attractive and a good mother, and Drake often regretted how things had turned out. He thought about her often. He knew she was trying to move on with a new relationship, with a guy by the name of Ted Iversen, but he also knew that it wasn't quite working out. He could see it in her eyes, in their watery sparkle, in the way the lines in her forehead seemed to smooth out and disappear, and in the way her eyebrows arched upward, welcoming him. Just like when they were together. Yes, he was glad to see her.

"You're here," Karen said.

"I am."

"I knocked."

"Sorry, the words were flowing. I couldn't stop."

She looked at him, appeared surprised. "Wow. It's going well?"

"It is. I woke up this morning, and I *had* to sit down and write."

"When was the last time that happened?"

"A long time ago."

"How long have you been working?"

Drake looked at the wall clock again, then he looked at his watch. He tapped the crystal of the watch with his finger and was still surprised at the lapse of time. "About five hours."

Karen nodded, was impressed. "I had to come into the city for an appointment. I brought your mail." She walked toward him and set the mail down on the desk. "You would think that after a year, they'd stop delivering your mail to the house. There's a bill there that you'll want to submit an address change for, so you can pay it on time."

"I'll take care of it right away," he said, which was a lie. He hoped to maintain the mail connection—to his house, his family—for as long as possible, for it made him feel that their relationship was not completely over. The change of address could wait. "You left the door open, do you have to run?" He hoped she could stay.

"Oh, I guess I did," she said. She looked back toward the open doorway and cleared her throat in a loud, exaggerated manner. She waited. "Samantha!"

Drake heard footsteps scurrying down the hallway, and he watched as his daughter, Samantha, ran up to his desk.

"Hi, Daddy. I was playing with the dog down the hall."

"Hi, baby. Get over here and give me a hug."

Samantha walked around his desk and sat in his lap. She put her arms around his neck and hugged him.

Drake squeezed her and held her tight. "So good to see you."

"Good to see you," she said. She loosened her grip, leaned backward, and studied his face. "You look tired."

"How come you're not in school?"

"It's Saturday."

"Hmm." Drake thought about the lapsed days. "So it is," he said, not convinced. "Where's your sister?"

"Soccer practice. Then she's going over to Amanda's house. We'll get her later."

"Well, stand up, and let me have a look at you."

It had only been a few days, maybe a week, since he had seen her but she looked different, older. Samantha was twelve years old and a spitting image of her mother, shorter in height but with identical facial features and similar mannerisms. She wore blue jeans and white Keds sneakers, along with an autumn-colored sweater—pumpkin, Drake thought—with the collar of her white shirt sticking out. And she appeared happy with her always-present smile.

"Why don't you go and pull out the craft box, you know where it is, and take it over to the dining table."

"Craft box? Daddy, I'm twelve."

"I know, but I need to talk with Mom."

"Okay."

Drake looked at Karen. Her arms were folded across her chest. She looked around the room, studied the surroundings, and shook her head. He could see she was not overwhelmed with or surprised by the condition of the place.

"You didn't have to make a special trip," he said.

"I know," she said softly, looking over to the dining table to make sure Samantha was preoccupied, "but for some reason, I still care. You're still the father of our children and I . . ." She stopped and smelled the air then crunched up her face as though she was repulsed.

Drake noticed. "What?"

She leaned closer. "Cigarettes and sex. You're really enjoying the bachelor life, aren't you?"

"You kicked me out."

"You were gone long before I kicked you out."

Drake didn't argue, couldn't argue, and he shrugged in confirmation.

"Are you seeing someone?" she asked.

He didn't say anything, didn't care to get into a discussion about his relationships. He watched as Karen walked over to the windows, and he swiveled in his chair, tracking her. He was still attracted to her, an attraction to her smile and laugh and sincere generosity that he felt as a twinge in his stomach and that was as strong as the day he first met her, and it seemed to him that it was not quite that long ago. She stopped before the windows and looked down on the street below. She backed up and inspected the panes of glass, which were haze-dirty from the elements both inside and out. She swiped a finger across one of the panes and realized that much of the dirt was on the inside. With her index finger she made a smiley face on the pane and underneath it, she wrote: WASH ME!

"The cleaning crew comes tomorrow," Drake said.

Karen reached into her purse and pulled out two hand-made greeting cards. She fanned them out, showing them to Drake as she walked over to hand them to him. "From the girls."

He took both cards and read each one, slowly, not wanting to miss out on the meaning, actual or implied, of each word. He studied the accompanying drawings, each made with colorful inks and reflecting a home-like scene of a happy family that included him. He realized how much he missed the girls' smiling faces and warm embraces, felt the realization in his gut, and he choked up with a lump in his throat.

He looked over at the dining table where Samantha sat, then looked at the picture frame on his desk, a single frame with two matted cutouts and current school pictures of his daughters. A picture of his younger daughter, Kelly, was on the left. She was ten, and while she also showed the same physical features of Karen and Samantha, Kelly took the opportunity, whenever she could, to be different. She wore her hair shorter, more of a boy's cut, and was confident and forward, more outgoing with whomever she met. She was into sports while Samantha was into books. In her school picture, Kelly wore her green and white soccer jersey while Samantha and most everyone else at the school had worn his or her uniform shirt.

Drake looked at the picture of Samantha on the right, her long and straight dark hair that hung down over her shoulders, the bangs draped across her forehead, her sparkling eyes, and her bright smile.

More so than screwing up his marriage, Drake regretted the impact the divorce had had on the girls. They seemed to have adjusted to and accepted the situation, but he knew it had to be hard on them. He still tried to make it up to them at each visit, giving his undivided attention for the scant hours he was with them and making his daughters' interests the sole priority of his visit.

He closed his eyes and pictured in his mind the last visit with them. He thought about their two smiling faces, the spitting images of their mother, and their goodbyes, which were always the same and almost a tradition now. He would hug both of them at the same time and ask, "Are you my big girls?" They always replied, "Yes, Daddy," in unison before kissing him on opposite cheeks, and then he would be gone.

He set the cards on the desk and looked up at Karen.

"They adore you," she said.

"And you?"

"I used to. Now, it's complicated."

Complicated indeed. He stood up from his chair and walked past her and over to the couch. He picked up his jacket, felt for the inside pocket, and pulled out his envelope of cash. Without counting, he separated off a nice stack of bills then threw his coat and the envelope back onto the couch. He walked over and handed her the money.

"What's this?" She counted the crisp bills.

Drake watched her facial expression change from surprise to concern.

"Did you rob a bank?"

"I have a job."

"A job? What about your book?"

"It's a short-term gig, an opportunity I couldn't pass up . . . and the book is coming along just fine." He walked back over and sat in his desk chair then leaned back and folded his hands in his lap, indifferent and sure of himself.

She stared at him, eyebrows raised.

He could tell she did not believe him. "What?"

Again, so Samantha could not hear, she leaned in close and said, "Our marriage ended because of your writing career. You better not be giving up on it now."

"Really, it's fine. I'll be done with this other job in a couple of weeks."

"What kind of job is it?"

Drake looked at her, his eyebrows came together and his eyes squinted, but he did not respond.

"You'd have to kill me?"

"You know me well."

She held the money out for him. "I can't take this."

"You can, and you will," he said. "It's just a little research assignment, for someone I had worked with back at the newspaper."

Same expression. She still did not believe him.

Drake said, "Honest. Take the money. Buy the girls something nice."

"Are you planning to come by soon? Kelly was sad she couldn't come with us today."

"Soon."

"And the book?"

"Like I said, I've been at it for five hours straight. I'm on a roll." He felt good about what he had accomplished. Add to that a nice visit from Karen and his daughter. It was a good day all around. "Hey, I don't think I told you. I spoke to Barbara a few days ago. She sold my next book."

She looked at him, eyebrows raised again. "Wow. When it rains, it pours. Congratulations." It seemed that was all she needed to hear, and she shoved the money into the front pocket of her jeans. "Samantha, did you hear that? Your father sold his newest book."

"Congratulations, Daddy," Samantha said without looking up from the table, in the midst of a creative flurry of her own.

Karen appeared contented. "Well then, I'll leave you to it." She stepped forward as if she was going to hug or kiss him but thought better of it and stopped. "You'll let me read it when you're done?"

"When it's done," he said.

"C'mon, Samantha, we need to let your father get back to work."

Samantha dropped the marker in her hand and picked

up her project, a single sheet of paper, and walked over to her father. "Here, Daddy, I made this for you."

Drake grabbed the sheet and turned it around to look at it. There on the page was Samantha's depiction of their family, each character drawn with elaborate detail, in descending sequence by height and with the appropriate label over its head—Daddy, Mom, Samantha, and Kelly—with smiles on their faces and holding hands with each other. He looked at Samantha with watery eyes.

"Don't be sad," she said.

"I'm okay, baby, now that I've seen you."

"Don't worry. Everything will turn out just fine." She put her arms around his neck, put her mouth up to his ear, and whispered, "And Mom still loves you." She let go of him and stepped back, a huge grin on her face.

Drake wiped a finger along the corner of his eye, and she winked at him.

"I love you," he said.

"Love you too." She went to her mother and grabbed her hand. "See you soon!"

"See you soon." He watched them leave, heard the closing of the door behind them, and he was, again, left alone with his most necessary and welcomed writing requirements: solitude and silence.

Drake slid his chair up to the desk and returned to his work.

13

It had been a productive morning for Drake, and his output continued into the afternoon. Most important, he had been able to break through his self-imposed creativity barrier, which was brought on by doubt, overthinking, and excessive alcohol consumption over the prior weeks. He had used the events of the last few days as an impetus for starting his new story and hoped that once he began, the story might take off and grow with less mental strain. His plan had worked.

Drake scrolled back up to the title page and read the three lines he had typed there earlier that afternoon. His novel was no longer "soon to be named." The story idea and plot had solidified in his mind and he had decided upon a fitting title.

A FINE LINE
A Jack Cannon Novel
By Sebastian Drake

He scrolled down to the next page and continued reading.

For some people, a job is a means to an end, a paycheck to cover the next bill or pay for the next unnecessary thing at the top of a long list of purchased items, all of them ultimately discarded to make room for the next one and all acquired in a fruitless effort to satisfy unrealistic material dreams before death.

For others, the job is the point of it all, the reason for living and getting up in the morning and the vehicle for getting out into the crazy world to make a difference.

For Jack Cannon, the job was everything.

Spending the last two weeks on administrative leave was no picnic for Cannon, sitting at home and wondering about his future with the Chicago Police Department. After nineteen years on the job, years of total and unbridled commitment "To Serve and Protect" and remove the human trash from the streets of Chicago, he was now suspended, awaiting the results of a full investigation concerning his recent shooting.

The incident had happened two weeks ago, yet the details remained vivid and disturbing in his mind. The call had come in at just after nine in the evening, a report of a man with a gun hiding out in an abandoned warehouse on the near West Side. Cannon and his partner had responded to the call and had entered the building with guns drawn. Inside, the building was dark, and Cannon led the way, searching by the beam of his flashlight. Cannon had taken the shot at precisely the moment he saw the silhouette of the man with his gun drawn and pointed at him. It had all happened so fast, and he had soon realized that the downed man was not a man at all but instead was a sixteen-year-old and somewhat mentally-challenged kid, and the gun the kid had pointed at him was a full-size automatic, black, and constructed of cheap plastic.

Over the following weeks, at the recurring thoughts of the young man and his mourning family, Cannon had worked himself into quite a depression. Even worse than the depression, if that were possible, was the thought of losing his job, as that would be unbearable, his life without meaning or purpose. But life turned around some, even if just a little, when an unexpected visitor showed up at his apartment this morning and offered him a job. The man said he had read about the unfortunate shooting in the newspaper and understood Cannon's predicament. I doubt it, Cannon had thought. But the man had explained his need for a private investigator to help with a stalled murder case, and though Cannon was not initially interested, the three thousand dollar retainer the man had left was enough to make him interested.

Funny how a day can change things, Cannon had thought after the man left. His depression lightened, and he decided he was not going to look lightly on what was clearly a good omen.

He was back in the game.

Drake read through the remaining pages he had written, then he worked on his story for another two hours, after which time he felt it was necessary to get out for some fresh air and to stretch his legs. He picked up a slice of pizza from the convenience store down the street and ate it, sitting at the curb, while he waited for a taxi to come by.

It was a short wait, and when the car arrived, he took a ride to the Chicago community of Bridgeport, a small residential area south of the city, about three miles away. Both Engel and Angie had suggested that Drake visit Billy Taylor, and he agreed it would be worth a visit and some discussion.

Drake had the driver stop in front of the grocery store on Ashland Avenue. He paid the driver, handed him an extra twenty dollars, and asked him to wait. The driver agreed, and Drake exited the taxi and walked into the front door of the store. He went straight to the customer service counter.

"Excuse me. Is Billy Taylor working today?"

The man behind the counter looked up and grumbled, appearing annoyed by the interruption. He scowled at Drake. He was maybe twenty-five and still struggled with a teenage complexion.

Drake looked up at the "Customer Service" sign, then down at the man, and wondered what the problem was. He waited for an answer.

"Aisle nine, I think," the man said while pointing. He looked down and returned to his unhappiness.

"Thanks," Drake said and headed in that direction. He walked down aisle nine toward a man who was kneeling on the floor, stacking cans on a shelf. The aisle was otherwise vacant.

"Billy Taylor?"

The man looked up at Drake but did not recognize him. His eyes were glassy and distant. He wore baggy jeans, a blue, collared shirt with the sleeves rolled up, and a red apron with a name tag that read: BILLY. Almost as a programmed response, he said, "Customer service is up front," then went back to stacking cans.

Drake thought the man appeared a bit slow, that the gears turned in his head with some difficulty, and he was a bit skittish, but he stacked the cans with near mechanical and stout precision. His concentration was so focused that the correct and straight display facing of the cans was all that seemed to matter. Drake could also tell that the man's whole life was likely his job at the store. He cared that much. It was probably his sole reason for getting up in the morning, his reason for being.

Drake tried again, "Excuse me, are you Billy Taylor?"

He finished placing a can on the shelf then stopped. He kept his gaze forward and stared at the cans. "Yeah, but I don't know you," he said. "I'm working. I need to do my job so I don't get fired."

"I'd like to talk to you for a minute."

"Go away. Please. You'll get me in trouble."

Drake looked around. The aisle was still vacant. He thought about his options. "Jack Mitchell sent me."

Billy looked up with surprise, recognized the name, and grinned wide. "The senator?"

"No, junior, the alderman."

Billy's grin disappeared. He stood up. "You know Mr. Mitchell?"

"I do."

"Who are you?"

"My name is Drake. I've been hired to look into the Sarah Mitchell murder."

Billy appeared concerned. He took a small step backward.

"Don't worry, Billy," Drake said. "This is just a routine investigation."

"You a cop?"

"Private investigator."

"The case is closed."

"Not any more."

Billy chewed a fingernail and looked around. Drake could see that his mind was churning, and he was uncomfortable with the news.

"You were a friend of Sarah Mitchell?" Drake asked.

Billy looked down at his shoes. "Yeah."

"Were you *good* friends?"

"*Best* friends."

"In a romantic way?"

Billy let out an uncomfortable laugh. "No, no, not like that. We'd been friends forever—since we were little."

Drake didn't say anything.

Billy let out another uncomfortable laugh. "What?"

"Does it bother you that they never found her killer?"

Billy thought about the question and grimaced. "Yeah, it makes me mad . . . *real* mad."

"Do you have any idea who did it?"

"Naw."

"Are you sure?"

Billy started to fidget and swayed back and forth while looking around. "I gotta get back to work."

"Just one more question."

Billy stared at Drake, nervously. "Did Mr. Mitchell really send you?"

"He did."

It appeared that Billy believed him, and he seemed to relax a little.

"Mr. Mitchell said that you're the one who did it—the one who murdered his sister."

Billy's face turned red and his eyes bulged. He gritted his teeth and pressed his lips together tight, and a deep growl rumbled in his throat.

Drake could see the anger rising within him, and after just a few seconds, he thought Billy was ready to explode.

"Liar! He did not! I did not! Take it back! That son of a . . . She was my friend . . . I loved—" He tried to calm himself, waited a few seconds, then said, "I would never do anything to harm her." He glared at Drake, breathing heavily. "For all I know, it was *him*."

"The alderman?" Drake asked.

Billy didn't say anything.

"What makes you say that?"

"Oh, I don't know." Billy regained his composure and looked down at his shoes again.

"Billy?"

He thought about his statement, about the question. He looked up. "He blames me; I blame him."

A middle-aged man dressed in a white shirt and tie came around the corner at the end of the aisle with a purposeful stride. Billy noticed, studied his shoes, and jammed his hands into the pockets of his jeans. Drake watched as the man approached, and he assumed by Billy's reaction that the man was the store manager or maybe his boss. The man stopped beside them. "Billy, is everything okay?"

Drake said, "I was just asking the young man if he could tell me where to find the canned asparagus."

"One aisle over, sir, in aisle eight," the store manager said.

"That's, that's what I told him," Billy said.

"Good, Billy." The store manager patted him on the shoulder. He said to Drake, "Sir, is there anything else we can help you find?"

"That's all. Thank you."

"You're welcome. Billy, finish up with that case then clean up the storeroom."

"Yes, sir."

Drake reached into his jacket pocket and pulled out a business card. He looked at it as though he was checking a shopping list.

The store manager walked away. Billy watched him turn the corner then breathed a sigh of relief.

"Thanks for your help," Drake said. He handed the card to Billy. "If you think of anything important that might be helpful to the investigation, please call me."

Billy took the card, looked at it suspiciously, and read it. "Writer? I thought you were a private investigator?"

"I am," Drake said.

"Which?"

"Both."

Billy scratched his head.

"It's a cover. I don't like people knowing that I'm a private dick."

"A dick?"

"Investigator, a private investigator."

Billy thought about what Drake had said, but it didn't

appear to register. He read the card again then put it into his pants pocket. He shook his head, knelt back down, and continued to stack cans as though the actions of the last few minutes never happened.

"Anyway, thanks for your time," Drake said as he turned and walked away down the aisle.

Outside and in front of the store, Drake took out a cigarette and lit it, replaying in his mind the discussion with Billy. It was clear that Billy had quite different and opposing feelings for the senator and the alderman, and Drake was curious about what had transpired to make him feel that way. He smoked and made a mental note to explore those relationships further. The sun was still high enough in the sky to warm his face, so he decided to enjoy the moment and finish his cigarette. The taxi was still idling in front of the store. Drake could see the driver leaning over and looking at him with an expression of *let's go* on his face, but Drake felt the man could wait. The driver leaned on the horn hard, and Drake heard him yelling something—words indecipherable and likely unflattering— through the closed car windows.

Drake reached into his pocket, pulled out a twenty-dol- lar bill, and waved it at the taxi driver, intent on finishing his smoke.

14

Drake had one other stop planned before heading back home. He snubbed out his cigarette, stepped back into the taxi, and handed the driver the twenty-dollar bill, which seemed to calm him some. He told the man to drive to the Whispering Heights Retirement Community, which was about an hour away up on the north shore in the town of Glencoe. Whispering Heights was a fairly new retirement living center that catered to the wealthy, and Drake was surprised when the taxi driver pulled away without having to punch a name or an address into the car's GPS.

Drake assumed his driver would take them out of Bridgeport and on to I-90, heading north then west to I-94 and staying away from the congested downtown area, so he leaned forward and asked the man if he would be so kind as to take the eastern route, up Lake Shore Drive and then Sheridan Road as far as he could go. The driver turned his head and looked at Drake as though he was insane—likely because of the time of day and the expected rush hour traffic on the smaller roads—and mumbled something to himself.

Drake said, "It's a nice day," as he threw a one-hundred-dollar bill onto the front seat.

The driver stopped mumbling.

They drove up Lake Shore Drive, heading north toward the downtown area. The ride was relaxed for a short time until the road swelled with crawling cars. Drake didn't mind the slow pace and enjoyed the views of the lakeshore from his rear seat window: the empty sands of the scruffy 31st Street Beach, the majesty of the Field Museum and the Adler Planetarium in the background, the Navy Pier Ferris Wheel, joggers and cyclists getting in an afternoon workout along the paved path at Oak Street Beach, a lonely fisherman casting for Coho salmon in the South Lagoon of Diversey Harbor, and the seemingly endless choppy waters bouncing up on the lakeshore rocks and leading out to neighboring states. Once on Sheridan Road, the traffic lightened. He especially enjoyed the ride when they made it to Evanston and drove past his alma mater, Northwestern University, a gem of a campus snuggled between Lake Michigan and an upscale residential neighborhood in Evanston. He had not been up that way for many years, and the memories of his time there came rushing back. *Yes, those were good times.*

* * *

Back in his junior year at Northwestern, enrolled as an undergraduate journalism major in the Medill School of Journalism, Drake had come across a flyer hanging on a bulletin board in the student commons advertising *The Target Club. Set your sights high*, the flyer stated. *Gun skills for a '10' in life and on the range. Sponsored by Sigma Phi Epsilon.* Drake never had any interest in the fraternity life on campus, but he had always wanted to learn how to shoot a gun, a skill his father—a marksman shooter while in the service and an avid gun collector—never felt comfortable passing along to his son. "You just worry about your grades," his father had always said when Drake brought up the topics of guns and shooting. Drake was intrigued and thought a visit to The Target Club might be fun. He tore off one of the perforated tabs from the bottom of the flyer, called the number, and obtained the details for the club's next meeting.

He learned that the club had been started by two young men from the fraternity who had a passion for handguns and the sport of target shooting. The father of one of the club's founders owned a shooting range located just across the border in Wisconsin, and a week later, Drake hitched a ride with three other guys in the club and had his first exposure to a handgun. Each club member had his own gun and was more than willing to let Drake have a try, and some of them were kind enough to provide him with some basic instruction.

Drake tried the many different guns and was hooked. He loved the feeling of the heavy and cold steel in his hands and the force and power the gun expelled with each pull of the trigger. He also loved the power the gun instilled in him, and it wasn't long before he had purchased his own pistol, a Smith & Wesson .38-caliber revolver.

Drake attended the next two club meetings, then he started going to the range on his own. Every minute he wasn't studying, he was thinking about shooting, and every cent that was not necessary for sustenance, he allocated for ammunition and

range time. It wasn't long until he was showing up at the range
with his fellow club members and winning their informal
competitions. He was a natural, and his extra practice was
returning dividends.

Unbeknownst to Drake and most of the other club
members, the range owner maintained an extensive contact
network of military and government personnel—people
who visited the range regularly and with whom he had
developed personal relationships. One of his regular customers, a full-bird colonel in the U.S. Marines and a fine
shooter in his own right, was always inquiring about who
the best or most proficient shooters were.

About six months after the day he first picked up a gun,
Drake was at the range, practicing, when Colonel Roger
Masterson approached him as he exited the live range area.
He told Drake he had been observing his shooting practice
and was impressed with his clear and comfortable skill with
a handgun. He also mentioned to Drake that he had a friend
in the U.S. government, no further specifics provided, who
was looking for an intern, someone to help test ammunition.
The colonel shared more of the details: a part time job to
participate in target practice, all the free ammo he could
shoot, and a paycheck. Drake felt it sounded too good to
be true.

It wasn't a decision that required much thought, and he
reported for work the next week.

* * *

When they arrived at Whispering Heights, just over an hour
since they had left the store, the drill was the same. Drake

paid the driver his fare, asked him to wait, gave him an additional twenty, and exited the taxi.

Drake had paid attention when they drove in through the front entrance of the property. He had noticed the two heavy iron gates that met and locked in the middle, swinging inward to allow entry, and the sentry house on the left side with an armed guard who asked for identification, inspected the car, and made note of the license plate number. Drake was impressed.

Now, inside the grounds and standing at the curb, he took a moment to look around and was further impressed by the estate-like facilities. In front of him was a long and wide one-story building, about a block long. It looked like the main building, constructed of brick and stone with a pitched roof that had dormers jutting out along the front side. Three five-story buildings, also brick but with flat roofs, were connected to the main building. Common services in the middle, residences in the attached buildings, Drake assumed. To his left was a park area with benches and outdoor games that were shaded by huge oak trees. Behind the park area was a golf course, which swung around behind him and went off into the distance. To the right of the buildings was a large parking lot, and on the other side of it was a hefty building that looked like it housed maintenance equipment.

Money.

Drake strode up the paved walkway and entered the front door of the main building. Once inside, he proceeded straight ahead to the security desk.

Two security officers sat behind the desk, and the one on the left looked up and acknowledged him. "May I help you, sir?"

"I'm here to see Senator Mitchell."

"ID, please."

Drake pulled out his wallet, removed his Illinois driver's license, and handed it to the officer.

The security officer inspected the license then typed Drake's name and driver's license number into the computer. He handed the license back. "Mr. Drake, the senator has been expecting you."

Drake was surprised and wondered how the senator could have known about his visit.

The security officer rose behind the desk. "If you'll follow me, please. He's just finishing his dinner."

Drake followed the security officer down the hall. At an open glass doorway, the officer turned right and led Drake into the common dining area. The room was a large and well-appointed area, much like a fine restaurant with neutral-colored walls, luxurious carpeting, and simple yet elegant chandeliers hanging from the ceiling. There were two dozen tables draped with white tablecloths, surrounded by high-back chairs, and set with fine china and silver. The wall that spanned the full length of the far side of the room was made entirely of glass, which allowed the diners to look out onto the landscaped and manicured grounds.

A woman greeter stood behind a high desk to the left of the entrance door. She was proper and attentive, and she noticed them as they entered. "Good evening," she said to Drake.

The security officer said, "This gentleman is here to see Senator Mitchell."

"Mr. Drake, the senator is expecting you."

Drake, surprised again, felt her comments were strange and the whole situation a bit disconcerting.

The woman said, "If you'll please follow me." She left the desk and walked down the aisle and along the left side of the room.

Drake followed her. The security officer left them and walked back to his station.

The woman slowed her pace and allowed Drake to catch up beside her. "Senator Mitchell has been diagnosed with Alzheimer's. Most of the time, he does not know or remember any of his visitors, and he tends to be stuck in an earlier time, in the distant past. Don't be alarmed."

Drake nodded.

"Surprisingly, today he is very lucid. He's been talking about your meeting all day."

"Why is it surprising?"

"Oh, it's just that he's been the same way for so long now. It's just great to see him like his old self."

"What caused the improvement?"

"Oh, I couldn't say. You'd have to ask his doctor, or, more appropriately, his family." She led him to the far side of the room, where an older man was seated at a corner table.

Drake recognized Senator Mitchell as they approached him. The senator was eighty-one years old, but Drake thought he looked a good ten years younger in person, because of the smooth and clear complexion of his youthful-looking face. He was dressed in gray slacks, an open collared white shirt, and a navy blazer. Drake thought they must allow the residents to get outside and walk the grounds regularly, because the senator was tanned and looked physically fit. He had neatly combed white hair, which was perfect and likely well attended to by an on-site stylist. He was dignified in every way, and Drake could tell he still commanded respect. The senator saw them approaching and acknowledged them with a wave.

"Senator Mitchell, this is Mr. Drake."

The senator remained seated but extended a hand.

Drake reached across the table and shook hands with the senator.

Senator Mitchell said, "Please excuse me for not getting up."

"Of course, Senator," Drake said. "It's a pleasure to meet you."

"The pleasure is mine. Please have a seat and make yourself comfortable."

Drake pulled out the chair across from the senator and sat down. They each made eye contact and smiled cordially.

Senator Mitchell turned to the woman and said, "Thank you, Sherri."

"You're very welcome, Senator," she said, then excused herself.

The senator turned back to Drake. "She's a good kid."

Drake looked at the woman walking away, whom he felt had to be at least forty years old and was not quite a "kid."

"Mr. Drake, thank you for coming to visit with me today. Can I offer you something to drink? Before you answer, I must tell you that, unfortunately, the bar is dry. It seems there is too much medication floating around to even allow for a small glass of wine, which I would die for right now—figuratively, of course. But we have great coffee."

Considering the hour, his day of activity, and the restaurant-like environment of his current engagement, Drake would have preferred bourbon. "Coffee is fine."

The senator flagged down a waiter, who hurried over and poured Drake a cup of coffee. He refilled the senator's cup and moved on to the next table.

"Did she tell you that I'm nuts?"

"No, she didn't."

The senator stared at him, did not believe his reply. He waited a moment. "If we're going to have any kind of relationship, I'll need you to be honest."

"She explained your condition."

"It's not as bad as it sounds," the senator said with a wave of his hand.

Drake didn't respond but raised his eyebrows.

"You don't believe me."

"I believe you."

They looked at each other, each trying to study and assess the other's situation.

Senator Mitchell said, "Three years ago, I started to forget things." He paused, considering his words as he rubbed his chin. "Does that ever happen to you?"

"I can't remember yesterday."

The senator appeared amused. "I'd wake up some mornings to find a strange woman in my bed." He laughed. "I could have worse problems, huh?"

"I suppose."

"Don't get me wrong. It was always my wife, there in the bed. I just didn't know it."

"I understand."

"I guess it became an issue when I started to get lost. I've always had a driver, still do, but there were times that, for some reason, I'd decide to go off on my own and end up fifty miles from home, penniless, clueless . . . lost . . ." The senator, now silent and reflective, looked off into the distance.

After an uncomfortable amount of time passed, Drake said, "Senator?" There was no response. "*Senator*," he said again, louder.

The senator snapped out of his trance and turned back to Drake. "Mr. Drake, how nice of you to join me."

Drake took a sip of coffee then set the cup down. "It's my pleasure."

The senator raised his cup and sipped, still trying to clear the fog. "Where were we?"

"You were telling me about the facility here."

"Yes, yes. It's the best facility in the state, maybe the country. We have five-star accommodations, world-class dining, and the best doctors."

Drake observed the impressive room. "Sounds nice."

"It costs a small fortune, but what the hell." He stared at Drake, smirking. "I have no one else to leave my money to." When he saw no reaction from Drake, he said, "Anyway, I know quite a bit about you, Mr. Drake."

"Is that so?"

"Yes, yes, but we'll get to that later. What do you know about me?"

"You've been in politics for fifty years," Drake said, "most recently as a senator of the great state of Illinois." He took another sip of coffee.

The senator waited a few seconds but became impatient. "C'mon, that's it?"

"You're an intelligent, successful man. Your life is a true rags-to-riches story. You grew up on the north side of Chicago, had a successful political career, and are well known throughout the state and across the country. I'd say you're possibly the nicest man in the world, always making the effort to help others less fortunate than yourself. You're retired now, living in an exclusive retirement home." Drake waved a hand, showing off the room. "And you are struggling with Alzheimer's."

"Impressive, although I wouldn't say I'm struggling. When it happens, I don't even realize it." The senator spoke the words matter-of-factly, as if his condition had no impact on him whatsoever. "Please, continue."

Drake said, "You've made every decision in your life for and by yourself, except for the one that landed you in this current predicament, in this place."

"You are correct."

"Which, I could imagine, might make you frustrated, angry, resentful."

Senator Mitchell waved off the last comment. "I'm fine, really. Actually, I'm more than fine. They started me on a new medication yesterday."

"Is that so. Who prescribed it—the new medication?"

"My doctor, I assume." The senator pointed toward his head. "It seems to have cleared the fog a bit." He thought about his statement and stared at his coffee cup.

"Senator, I've been hired to look into your daughter's murder case."

The senator looked up, his eyes now glazed, trying to process the statement. "The case? The case is closed."

"Not anymore."

"I see."

"Is there anything you can tell me, anything that might shed some new light on the case?"

The senator did not need to think about his answer. "It seems I've been through it a thousand times, played it over, time and again, in my mind. I told the authorities everything I know."

"Of course you did."

"I cooperated fully."

"I know."

The senator stared off into the distance again.

Drake realized he was losing him. "Senator?" There was no response. "*Senator.*"

The senator looked at Drake, without recognition. "Yes, yes, Mr. —"

"Drake."

"Yes, Mr. Drake. I know all about you."

"You said that before. What have you heard?"

"Yes, yes, we'll get to that later."

"Senator, can I ask you a question?"

"Of course."

"What was your relationship to Police Chief Taylor?"

The senator pondered the question; his eyes squinted and eyebrows furrowed in concentration. "He was a good man, served the City of Chicago well. He was a neighbor and a friend." He looked up at the ceiling, thoughtful. "Always by-the-book . . . well, most of the time." He looked at Drake again. "He would do anything for me, and I would do anything for him."

"What about his son, Billy?" Drake asked.

"What about him?"

"I understand he might have information that is relevant to the case."

"Nonsense."

"Senator?"

"That is nonsense, Mr. Drake. I'm sure you have read the case file. The young boy was devastated by the loss of his friend. That's all."

"I also understand that he came forward, wanting to help with the investigation."

"Mr. Drake, we're talking about a fifteen-year-old boy, at the time, with a significant learning disability, traumatized by a horrendous murder. Chief Taylor felt the need to protect his boy from any further emotional trauma." The senator sipped his coffee while maintaining eye contact with Drake. "And I agreed. There was no point, no benefit, in torturing the boy any further."

Drake said nothing.

The senator's eyes glazed over again, became watery. "I believe Chief Taylor is coming to visit today."

"Unfortunately, Senator, he passed away three years ago."

The senator processed the statement but did not react. "I believe you are correct. That little fact seemed to have slipped my mind." The senator looked toward the greeter's station and waved his hand to get Sherri's attention.

Sherri noticed the senator waving and hurried over. "Yes, Senator?"

"Can you get Jerry on the line for me? Something has come up, and I need his assistance."

She looked at him, expressed discomfort and concern. "Senator?"

"Get him on the line . . . Tell him to meet me in the situation room right away."

Sherri looked at the senator, looked at Drake, then back at the senator, chewing the inside of her cheek and not sure what to do.

Drake watched her, felt her discomfort.

"That will be all. Thank you," the senator said. "Run along now."

"Yes, Senator," she said then hurried away.

"So, Mr. Drake, where were we?"

"You were going to tell me who murdered your daughter."

Senator Mitchell laughed. "I would if I knew, I assure you . . . and isn't that your job to find out?"

"It is. Can you help?"

"I would love to, but . . . It seems I've been through it a thousand times, played it over, time and again, in my mind." The senator looked toward the greeter's station again; his eyes were fixed, still glazed, and locked in on something.

Drake followed the senator's line of sight and saw a woman walking toward their table.

15

Clarisse Mitchell, Senator Mitchell's wife, approached the table with a determined stride then walked over and stood behind the senator. She put her hands on his shoulders, massaged him, and glared at Drake.

The report Engel had provided about her was thorough. Now sixty years old, Clarisse Mitchell had met the senator at a fundraising event years back when she was only thirty. He was fifty at the time, divorced with no children. Their two-month affair went straight to marriage once they learned that Clarisse was pregnant with their first child, Jack, Junior. Born of simple, small town means as an only child to fourth-generation farmers, Clarisse grew up quiet and studious and was kept under close and watchful eyes. In her twenties and after finishing college, she rebelled, becoming more outspoken and aggressive in her efforts to take on the world, to "get what she deserved," as she had put it, and she never looked back. She latched on to the senator and became the matriarch of the Mitchell family, willing to do anything to support her husband's political career and keep the family reputation untarnished. Engel's report even included several news articles that highlighted her best retaliatory quotes targeted at reporters and politicians who had the nerve to challenge her husband's credibility. She was now a well-respected family figurehead regularly seen in a custom-tailored wool suit. She was educated, proper, and soft-spoken but firm. She had a businesswoman's persona with a front of overt pleasantness, behind which there were likely secrets—as most people had—that no one was ever truly aware of, not even her husband. While polite, she always left a "do not mess with me" impression.

Drake was struck with that impression immediately upon seeing her.

"Hello, darling," Clarisse said to the senator. She bent down and kissed him on the cheek.

He looked up at her. "Darling." He waved his hand toward Drake. "Clarisse, this is Mr. Drake. Mr. Drake, my wife, Clarisse."

Clarisse glanced down at the senator, seemed surprised at the introduction. She massaged his shoulders again, bent down close to his ear, and whispered, still loud enough for Drake to hear, "Darling, you remember my name."

Drake stood up and extended a hand toward her. "Mrs. Mitchell, it's a pleasure."

She remained standing behind the senator, gave a cold reception, and did not acknowledge his gesture. "Mr. Drake, I understand you were just leaving."

Senator Mitchell said, "But we were—"

Clarisse stroked the senator's hair. "Darling, you've had a long day. It's time for you to retire for the evening."

"But I'm not—"

With both of her hands still on his shoulders, she massaged

him gently then a bit harder, cutting him off with her firm touch. "Mr. Drake is leaving, and I'm going to take you back to your suite."

Drake, still standing, realized the meeting was over. "Senator, it was a pleasure to meet you." He walked around the table and shook hands with him. "Maybe I can come by again some time."

"I would like that," the senator said.

Clarisse said, "I don't think that will be possible, Mr. Drake. The senator will not be seeing any more visitors. If you wouldn't mind, can you please see yourself out?"

"Of course," Drake said. He left the table, walked across the room, and glanced back. The senator and his wife watched him. The senator expressed resignation; she was concerned and watchful.

* * *

Drake passed the security station and exited the main building of Whispering Heights. The sun was setting, and the impending dusk made the grounds seem uninviting and cold, more like a cemetery than a resort. He raised the collar of his jacket to fend off the cold wind. His taxi was at the curb, waiting for him.

Behind the taxi, Drake saw a late-model Lincoln Town Car: black, with tinted windows, and spotless. The driver and front passenger doors opened, and two large and imposing men, dressed in matching black suits and wearing sunglasses, exited the car. *Bodyguards.* The man on the passenger side opened the rear door of the car and another man, whom Drake recognized, stepped out: Alderman Jack Mitchell, the senator's son. Drake knew of him by regular news reports, and Engel had provided some additional insight and perspective in his prepared materials. The alderman was thirty-one years of age, brash, and aggressive. Drake knew the alderman was on a power trip, seeking to realize grand political aspirations, whatever the cost. He assumed the alderman was the type of person who had never been told "no" and who always received, or took, everything he wanted, especially when it came to personal possessions and women. *Harvard educated and street stupid . . . a turd in a two thousand dollar suit,* Angie Parker had said.

Engel had provided details of the many deals the alderman had brokered between business leaders, himself, and other city officials. Some were questionable but never questioned. He was a politician quite different from his father. Polar opposites, one might say. Like many Illinois politicians who had ventured into inappropriate territory and had been caught and prosecuted, the alderman likely had a deep well of buried trouble, and it was just a matter of time until he was exposed. Drake thought it would be nice if he could help the alderman get the appropriate exposure.

As he stepped out of the car, the alderman looked around like he was attending a red carpet event, and Drake thought he might start waving. Instead, he made minor adjustments to his finely tailored and expensive suit so it felt and appeared just right before walking toward Drake, flanked by the bulging bodyguards who exhibited faces of rock. "So, you must be Mr. Drake."

"Alderman Mitchell," Drake said.

"You know who I am. I'm impressed."

Drake said nothing.

"Mr. Drake, would you mind if one of my men checked you for a weapon?

"I would."

"It's just a precaution. I assume the guards inside checked you, but, then again, it's so hard to find good help. You know, you can't be too careful these days."

The alderman and Drake stared at each other. The alderman became cocky with an inflated chest and nudged the bodyguard who was standing to his left. The bodyguard stepped forward and at three feet, he reached out at Drake aggressively in an attempt to frisk him. Before the bodyguard could make contact, Drake reacted. He shifted his weight with his own step forward, momentum into momentum, and jammed the heel of his left palm into the man's nose. Cartilage snapped, blood spurted, and the bodyguard froze momentarily before collapsing to the ground. Drake reached inside his jacket with his right hand and pulled his Walther from its holster and had the pistol sighted on the other bodyguard's forehead a second later.

Drake's steely gaze pierced the second bodyguard, who stiffened. The alderman grinned but was uncomfortable. The first bodyguard was down on one knee, blood dripping from his nose and on to the sidewalk.

Drake said to the standing bodyguard, "Why don't you help your friend here and take him back to the car."

The man tensed with anger, his face contorted.

Drake had the feeling that the guy might prefer to take his chances, go one-on-one with him, so he said, "Don't be a dummy."

The bodyguard's face flushed with rage, and he grunted and stepped forward.

The alderman reached over and set a hand on his arm. "I'll be fine. Go ahead. Help him back to the car."

Reluctantly, the bodyguard stepped back, walked behind the alderman, and went over to his associate, who was cupping his broken nose, blood dripping through his fingers. He helped him up with one arm and walked him over to the car. They looked back at Drake, angry and itching for another shot.

Drake smirked at them, winked, and put his gun back into its holster. "Cute couple."

The alderman grinned. "You're funny."

"Let me guess: your mommy called you."

"Yes, Mr. Drake, my mother called, and I just happened to be on my way. It's lucky for you that we should have the opportunity to meet."

"Yes, it is my lucky day."

"As you can likely understand, my mother is concerned about my father's well-being. We all are. He doesn't get many visitors, and we like it that way. Why are you here?"

"I've been hired to look into your sister's murder."

"That's interesting."

"It appears there is one person who is not convinced the case should be closed."

"And who might that be?"

"Actually, let's make it two," Drake said. "I'm not convinced either."

"I don't care if you're convinced or not. The case has been closed for a long time, and as difficult as it has been, our family has moved on."

"Maybe we could meet for a drink," Drake said. "I could ask you a few questions, write up my report, and be on my way."

"I don't think so."

"Did *you* do it?"

"Mr. Drake, your judo—or whatever you call it—and your gun do not scare me. I honestly believe that you do not know who you are fucking with, so I am going to cut you a break. Leave now, and don't ever come back here. I'll pretend like none of this ever happened."

Drake stood firm, undaunted, and did not respond.

"I know you realize that I am running for re-election and understand that the last thing I need is to have to deal with your ineptitude and any negative publicity resulting from your supposed investigation. If I find you're digging up the past and in any way publicizing anything that might disparage me or my family, I will—"

"Kill me?"

After a quick laugh, the alderman's grin was replaced with a solemn expression. He said, "That won't be necessary, Mr. Drake. I'm a very powerful man in this city. If need be, I'll deal with you in a much more humane, yet equally effective manner."

Drake felt that the alderman was a blowhard, and he was already bored with his comments. "Well, there's my taxi. Let me know if you want to have that drink." He walked toward the car, looked back, and the bodyguards tracked him, wishing they could pounce. The alderman, an expression of reserved concern on his face, watched Drake get into the taxi then watched the car drive away.

As the car pulled away from the curb, Drake glanced

out through the rear window and saw the alderman turn back toward his bodyguards, who were leaning against his car and collecting themselves. The alderman stared at them, hands on hips. He shook his head in disgust and walked up to the building entrance alone.

16

Later that evening, Drake was seated behind his desk, writing and smoking and drinking some bourbon. He realized he was most comfortable and felt the best when he was sitting at his desk, since it seemed it was the only place any true, productive, and meaningful actions transpired for him.

His desk was an executive-sized beast, made of solid oak and handcrafted in the early twentieth century by an artisan who cared. It was as big as a compact car and more than large enough for him to get lost behind. He had bought it fifteen years ago at a garage sale on the north side of the city for thirty-five dollars. The deal was a steal, he had thought, and a godsend for the seller who desperately wanted the junk removed from his yard. After he had refinished the wood and replaced the hardware with period-correct parts, the desk became one of his most prized possessions and the most important tool for his career, even more important than his computer or his journal.

He was invigorated and on a roll. The words were shooting from his brain to his fingers to the keyboard and to the digital page in a rapid fashion, line after line appearing before him on the computer screen. Smoke from the cigarette in the ashtray floated across his line of sight.

Drake had been working for a couple of hours and was pleased with his productivity. His writing had not come this easily for some time. Back when he was disciplined and writing well, he'd felt it was a good day if he could pound out a thousand words. He'd already written three thousand words in just this one day. All he knew was that while he couldn't explain it, he wasn't going to fight it. Over the years, he had come to realize that when the Muse finally arrived, however long it might have taken, he had to welcome her with open arms and embrace and hold onto her for as long as he could. It seemed she never stayed for long.

He couldn't explain it, the good fortune of words, and how or why it had happened was irrelevant. All that mattered was that it *had* happened. He felt revitalized, as if he had a direction and a purpose once again. *It's the case. There's something not right about it. The girl. The senator. Engel. Why was the case closed? Why did the past investigation fail? Somebody needs to avenge her death. All of it is making me think, which is good for a change, and that thinking is forcing me to sit down and write. Who would have thought? Engel.*

His new Jack Cannon story continued to formulate in his mind, and he typed at a feverish pace, fighting off the coming end of the inspiration he knew was imminent.

The phone on his desk rang. It startled and annoyed him all in the same moment. He ignored the first two rings, wishing he could let the call pass, but his concentration was broken. After taking a moment to read over the last sentence he had written and was comfortable that he knew how to continue when he returned to it, he picked up the phone. "Hello?"

"Mr. Drake, this is Thomas Engel. Do you have a moment?"

Drake looked at the computer screen, at the words. He wasn't sure that he wanted, could afford, to break away for long.

"Mr. Drake?"

Drake conceded. "Sure."

"I hope I am not interrupting anything important."

"Just the writing."

"You are writing," Engel said, as if he expected the outcome. "Well, that is good to hear."

"What can I do for you, Mr. Engel?"

"I thought this might be an appropriate time for an update on the status of your investigation."

"How about later?"

"I will have to insist that we do it now. I need to see that I am getting a return on my investment. Your next check is dependent upon it."

Drake, now feeling inconvenienced *and* manipulated, leaned back in his chair and took a swig of bourbon. He picked up his cigarette and drew on it hard. "I'm making progress."

"I understand you have met the police chief and some members of his team, and it seems your relationship with Detective Parker has proven beneficial."

Drake said nothing.

"You met with Mr. Taylor today, and earlier you returned from your meeting with the Mitchell family."

"It seems you're up to date."

"What is your assessment at this point?" Engel asked.

"It's too soon to say," Drake said, staring at the screen and trying to remember where he left off.

"Mr. Drake, I need to know."

Drake took another swig of bourbon, another drag from his cigarette. "Billy Taylor is an interesting character. He's bothered by something, and it's likely he has something more to say. The Mitchell family—let's just say they're unique. Surprisingly, the senator's condition has improved." *A coincidence?* "And it seems he has something he wants to get off his chest, although I'm not sure what it is yet. His wife, however, is extremely protective, and I think she will do whatever is necessary to ensure that nothing more is said. Junior, the alderman, is a real piece of work. Let's just say that I don't trust him."

"Did the senator say or provide anything useful?"

"We started with your normal pleasantries," Drake said, "and he seemed periodically distracted. Just before his wife arrived, he was talking about having a meeting in the situation room. It was odd."

"Did he mention any names?"

Drake took a moment, thought hard about the question, trying to understand what Engel was after.

"Mr. Drake?"

Drake replayed in his mind his meeting with the senator. *Can you get Jerry on the line for me? Something has come up, and I need his assistance.* Drake thought about the comment then said, "No. No names."

"Very well then," Engel said. "What is next?"

"I'd like to talk with the senator again. We were cut off

by his wife, and I just have this feeling that he wants to tell me something."

"A feeling?"

"The way he was acting: his attention, his sincerity, and his expressions. I could just tell."

"Very well."

"And in pursuing another discussion with the senator, I'm sure I'll have the pleasure of meeting with the rest of the family again. They're a close-knit and protective bunch."

"Mr. Drake, if you don't mind, I will check in with you again tomorrow, in person, at which time I can provide you with the retainer for your next week of services."

"I'll be here."

"Have a good evening, Mr. Drake."

Drake hung up the phone. He pulled the bottle of bourbon out from his desk drawer and refilled his glass. He lit a cigarette. After a gulp and a few drags, he went back to his story. It took a few minutes, but he was pleased once again when the rhythm came back. The protagonist of his story, Jack Cannon, was coming to life. With each new setting he created for Cannon, Drake was able to put himself into the head of his character and go along for the ride, to see what might happen. Sometimes, Drake led the way, but often he found Cannon going off on his own, doing and saying things that were so unlike Drake and so much like the new character he had created. *That's when the magic happens.* With each new step that Cannon took on his own, Drake felt excited, sometimes surprised, and always exhilarated. His fingers came alive, tapped the keyboard in a blur of activity. A smoky haze gathered around him as the words appeared across the screen, and he was immersed in his story again after the momentary distraction.

* * *

At about ten thirty that evening, Detective Parker drove past Drake's apartment, looked for a parking spot, and pulled up to the curb just down the street. She put the car into park, cut the engine, and took out a small, black notebook from her jacket pocket. She leafed through a few pages, stopped, and ran a finger over a couple of written lines as she squinted to read them, the dim cabin of her car lit only from the street-lights outside. She leaned over, opened the glove box, and tossed the notebook inside.

She sat for a moment, contemplating whether to get out or not, and sensed a nervous tingle in her stomach. Lights appeared in her side view mirror, and she watched them get closer. The car came into her vision on the left, passed her, and continued down the street. After checking the mirror again and seeing the empty street, she opened the door and stepped out. The street was silent, the air cool. She looked around, observant, while questioning herself about her reasoning for visiting Drake. She told herself, convinced herself, that it was all about the case and that she needed to see him and talk to him while her ideas were fresh in her mind. It was her job. That he was handsome and available were side benefits—maybe.

She locked the car door. Before she could move toward the apartment building, a black van rounded the corner, pulled up along side her, and stopped hard, brakes locked and screeching. As she turned around, the side door of the van opened and two men, dressed in black and wearing ski masks, grabbed her, put duct tape over her mouth, and pulled a black hood over her head. Their arms squeezed her like a vice, and she screamed and kicked to no avail. They threw her into the van like a rag doll, head first and with force, and she hit her head on something hard—metal—before rolling on the floor of the van and losing consciousness. Before everything went dark, she felt their hands on her, groping and searching. She heard the jingle of keys before the van door slammed shut and the vehicle sped away.

* * *

In his apartment, Drake was still typing away at his computer. An errant thought came to him, out of nowhere and while in mid-sentence, and he stopped typing as he looked around the room and considered the self-imposed interruption. He picked up the phone and dialed a number, listened, and after three rings, his call was answered.

"Hello?"

"Scotty, it's Drake."

"You're up late."

"Yeah, listen, I need you to look into another person for me."

"It's getting to be just like the old days. Shoot."

"All I have is a first name: *Jerry*. I met with Senator Mitchell today and he mentioned the name, in a way you would refer to . . ." Drake paused to recollect the words.

I need his assistance.

"Maybe a relative or staff member. Someone close, trustworthy. See if you can find anyone by that name who is in any way related to the Mitchell family."

"Will do," Scotty said. "Anything else?"

"I think that's all for now. Thanks."

"How's the investigation going?"

"It's a little too soon to say. Mr. Engel has certainly done his homework and has made my job quite easy so far, but . . ."

"What?"

"I can't put my finger on it right now, but I'm not sure about him. I'm getting that feeling . . ."

"That's not good," Scotty said.

"That's why I want you to look into this Jerry character. I didn't mention it to Engel, and I'd like to see what we can come up with on our own, before talking with Engel about him. Just as a precaution."

"Your gut and instinct have served us well in the past."

"Yeah. I know it's a lot to ask, but can you get on this right away?"

"Sure. I didn't feel much like sleeping tonight anyway. I'll call you tomorrow."

"Thanks," Drake said, and he hung up the phone. He lit a cigarette and smoked and thought more about the case as he reclined in his chair and gazed up at the ceiling, realizing he likely would not be sleeping much that evening either.

* * *

As a big man, it was reasonable for Drake's friend, Scotty, to think that an employer would target him for a job aligned with his physical skills and abilities. But Scotty always knew there were better options. Although he was an all-star linebacker in high school and loved to knock the snot out of an opposing player with a crushing blow, he was also an honors student with an unquenchable appetite for crunching numbers and conducting research, as hard to believe as that might be given his size and stature, since at that time he was six-foot-two and two hundred and thirty pounds. He also had an uncanny knack of adapting to the newest technological developments. He was a nerd, to be accurate, yet no sane person would ever consider using such an adjective to describe him—then or now.

Scotty spent four years at MIT on a full scholarship, the only stipulation being that he participate in a number of federally-funded research projects at the university. His experience there with the latest hardware technology and software tools was profound and set him on an accelerated curriculum specializing in data analysis and massively parallel processing technologies, the linking together of hundreds of microprocessors to break up a data query into parts and then process the parts simultaneously in a fraction of the time. At MIT, Scotty was using "big data" as input to his research, extensive amounts of data collected from Internet-connected devices and transactional systems, and performing specialized "data analytics" to conduct profiling studies on individuals, a good twenty years before the terms were coined as recent new technology developments in the business world.

In his senior year at MIT, his relationship with the CIA began when they had recruited him for a summer internship at the CIA headquarters in Langley, Virginia. They had big plans for Scotty, and after graduation he willingly accepted a position as a data analyst. He adapted quickly and became a sought-after resource for critical projects. He was known as the "answer man." He worked for the CIA for almost nine years before they considered him for an opportunity outside of the office, one that required firearms training and put him on a course to meet Drake.

Scotty had taken a liking to Drake upon their first meeting at their firearms training at Glynco, and their friendship was solidified from the start. Drake would tell you that the feeling was mutual. Each man had a distinctive background and set of personal qualities than the other, and Scotty was almost ten years older, but their fundamental beliefs regarding hard work and doing whatever was necessary to stand out among their peers were the same. They each understood that every person in their group was handpicked, the best of the best, but Drake and Scotty wanted to be better. Scotty saw the desire in Drake's actions, a desire just like his own. They paired together at every opportunity to push and challenge each other, and often at the end of the day's training, they would get together for a beer and talk about how they were going to approach the next day.

After their training was completed, they had each gone their separate ways, on to their own individual assignments. Scotty made an effort to keep in touch with Drake and maintain their friendship, and as most real friendships go, theirs flourished without the need for frequent interaction. If he were asked to pinpoint what it was that brought and kept them together as friends, Scotty would say that it was simply that they liked, respected, and trusted each other, and he knew that Drake felt the same way.

More than a year had passed before they had the opportunity to work together on an assignment. It was a chance pairing, each having been pulled from their isolated and distant department and job with an opportunity to work abroad. Their assignments were not mandatory, but each of them accepted upon learning the details and that the other would be involved.

On their first assignment together, a covert operation, as they unknowingly were about to walk into a hell storm of an ambush in a small town outside of Tehran, Drake's instincts about an informant—who had been turned and was working for the bad guys—proved correct. With the aid of some quick analytical work by Scotty, Drake took the lead and suggested—insisted upon—a change to their plans. His superiors back at base had agreed to his new plan, which had ended up saving both their lives, and from that point on, their trust in and reliance on each other was cemented.

Years later, after Drake had left the Agency, Scotty had tried to stay in touch, but Drake kept his distance, kept to himself, out of necessity for his personal well-being. Scotty understood, given the circumstances, and he knew he would be there for Drake whenever he decided to get back in touch again.

And he was very glad to see Drake when he walked into the shop the other day. Scotty knew that time had passed, but it did not matter, because when he saw Drake, he felt like he did back at their first meeting. Their friendship was still solid.

Drake was his friend. Scotty owed him and would do anything for him.

17

Drake awoke the next morning at nine, a bit sluggish. The night before, the words had come easily, and he added another three thousand of them to his story before retiring. He had found his sentences forming effortlessly, structure and sound coming together in a meaningful collaboration, in a manner that was suited to his story's protagonist, Jack Cannon. He had thought about Cannon, and the bourbon had flowed in celebration of his good fortune.

The sluggish feeling was not new but had relented recently. Prior to the last couple of days, he had been hitting the bottle hard for some time. He couldn't recall exactly when his drinking had escalated to a new level, but he knew he was in rare form right after the divorce. He also realized he had been a drinker since his college days, and although his ex-wife, Karen, never alluded to it, his drinking was likely one of the problems that led to her decision to divorce him. While his body had grown accustomed to a regular hangover, this morning it seemed less of an issue given his writing productivity the night before. Maybe, he thought, he was turning to a new page in his life.

After a shower and a quick breakfast, he left the apartment.

He exited the building and stopped just outside the entrance door where the mailboxes were recessed into the wall. He opened his mailbox, pulled out two envelopes, and scanned them. One envelope contained a bill, from the telephone company, which did not interest him. He recognized the return address on the other envelope, which did interest him. He opened the envelope and pulled out a single sheet letter and a check. The check was from his agent, The Barbara Sellers Literary Agency, and was made out to him in the amount of $10,625. He looked at the check, indifferent at first, but then thought *it's going to be a good day.*

He read the accompanying letter, written personally by Barbara, which explained that the check represented fifty percent of the advance from Random House, less her fifteen percent commission. The publisher would deliver the other half of the advance upon receipt of his manuscript, which, she reminded him, was due at the end of next month. The letter was signed in ink, and below her signature, Barbara had scribbled: *Now the pressure is off. Just write.* He folded the letter and stuffed it, along with the check, back into the envelope. Then he put both envelopes into the breast pocket of his jacket. He looked into the mailbox again and noticed something else. He reached in and pulled out a set of car keys, held them and looked at them. He weighed them in his hand, wondered where they came from, then he shrugged and put them in his jacket pocket and re-locked the mailbox.

He descended the steps and walked down the street toward his bookstore. Still thinking about the keys, he unknowingly walked past Angie Parker's parked car, but ten feet farther down the sidewalk, he stopped and turned back and looked at it. He vaguely recognized the car but thought nothing more of it and continued down the street.

As he approached the entrance of his bookstore, his phone rang. He looked at the caller-ID and took the call. "Hello, Barbara."

"That's much better, darling," she said. "Do you have a minute for your wonderful agent?"

"Of course."

"You sound happy."

Drake was thinking about the keys in his pocket.

"Drake?"

"I'm here."

"I just called to see if you received your check."

"I did. Thank you."

"I had it sent over, for delivery yesterday. I didn't hear from you."

"I've been busy."

"*Are* you happy?"

"The check's a little short."

"You know the drill: twenty-five thousand—half now, half when they get the book—less my hard-earned fee. You have to admit, my fifteen percent fee is well worth it."

Drake thought about that.

"Drake?"

"I appreciate you, and your fee," he said.

"Thank you, darling. So, tell me, how is the book coming along?"

The words registered, and Drake's attitude changed. He felt like talking. "Good, actually. I'm on a roll. I've been more productive in the last two days than I've been in the last two months. Maybe the last two years."

"That's wonderful. Great news. When will it be finished?"

"It's a little too soon to say."

"Go ahead, you can say."

"You'll have it in time, by the end of next month, don't worry."

"Are you writing today?"

"I will, later."

"Drake?"

He didn't respond.

"Drake, I told Random House you would make their problem go away, that you would deliver the final book of their spring lineup. They're counting on you. I'm counting on you."

"Relax, Barbara. You'll get your book."

"Okay, darling. Keep at it. If you find yourself with a break in the action, call me, and I'll come to Chicago and buy you a drink."

"I'll talk to you soon," Drake said, and he ended the call. He realized the time frame Random House had set was tight, but he was comfortable he could make the deadline. He rubbed the front of his jacket, felt the envelopes in the inside pocket—the check—and that made him feel better. He entered the building and took the elevator up to the second floor.

When he walked into the bookstore, he found Rita at the front counter, on the phone and appearing concerned. She noticed him, and he could see that she was relieved by his arrival.

Into the phone, Rita said, "Excuse me, he just walked in."

She held the phone close to her chest. "Drake, it's Mr. Engel," she said in a hushed voice. "You need to take this." She held out the phone to him.

Drake approached the counter and took the phone from her, annoyed at the early morning interruption by Engel. He spoke into the phone, an edge in his voice: "Mr. Engel, I know you're anxious, but not much has happened since we spoke last night."

"Actually, Mr. Drake, quite a bit *has* happened."

"Is that so?"

"I have a reliable source who informed me that a woman was found washed up on the bank of the Chicago River. He believes it is the body of Detective Angie Parker."

Drake was caught completely off guard by news he never would have expected. His stomach tightened and jaw muscles tensed. He tried to process and make sense of the words.

"Mr. Drake?"

Drake said nothing.

"Mr. Drake, are you there? Did you hear me?"

Drake felt his demeanor and his expression transform as Rita watched him. Anger welled up in his chest, and it felt like a truck had parked on it. A simmering rage he had not felt for some time overcame him. "I heard you," he said. "Who is your reliable source?"

"That is not important."

"WHO IS YOUR SOURCE," Drake shouted, which made Rita jump and step back from the counter. She looked at him, scared.

"I cannot divulge that information, Mr. Drake."

Drake took a deep breath in an attempt to maintain his composure. "Where?"

"The Canal Street Marina—2059 S. Canal."

Drake stared at the wall behind Rita, and his vision blurred as he mentally recorded the address and tried to visualize the location. He was familiar with the area but had not been around there in some time. The marina was located in a sparsely populated industrial area on the South Branch of the Chicago River, part of a network of waterways that cut through the city and, while it was once a corridor of commercial activity and provided a link from Lake Michigan to the Mississippi, the river now served as thoroughfare for sightseeing cruises and recreational boats. The marina was a little less than two miles south and a quarter mile west from where he was. He slammed the phone down onto the counter, startling Rita again, and headed for the door.

"Drake? Is everything okay?"

Without turning around, he said, "I'll be back later." He left the bookstore and, in the interest of time, hurried down the stairwell to the first floor.

* * *

Drake was lucky to catch a taxi coming down the street as he exited the building. It was a ten-minute ride over to the marina, longer than expected because the driver was not familiar with the area and there was some traffic. The ride was just long enough for Drake to anguish over the possibility that Angie was dead. He wondered about what might have happened. *It has to be a mistake. Was it an accident, or was there foul play?*

The taxi pulled up and stopped at the marina entrance. Drake fished out a ten-dollar bill from his pocket and paid the driver. Across the marina parking lot, he saw two unmarked police cars and a wagon marked COOK COUNTY MEDICAL EXAMINER. Drake stepped out, and the car pulled away fast, spitting gravel at his legs. Drake didn't care, was in a zone. He scanned the area and saw a lot of gravel, a few weeds poking up through the ground, and garbage blowing around like tumbleweeds. He again observed the medical examiner and police vehicles then gazed off beyond the marina buildings to where the river flowed. A strong, cold wind blew across the lot and sent a chill up his spine. He raised the collar of his jacket and walked across the marina lot toward the cars and people.

Drake recognized Detective Hartman, who was standing beside two men in street clothes. They were all looking down at the ground solemnly and not speaking. A man with one knee on the ground and MEDICAL EXAMINER emblazoned on the back of his dark blue jacket was zipping up a white body bag.

Drake approached them and caught a glimpse of what he thought was Angie's face as the medical examiner zipped the bag closed. He wasn't sure because the face he saw, while he could tell it was a woman's face, was blue and lifeless, hair pasted against her face like matted seaweed.

Drake had seen worse, but nonetheless, he reacted with disgust and felt a burning sensation in his chest.

Hartman looked up, saw Drake, and approached him. "What the fuck are you doing here?"

"What happened?"

"I asked you a question," Hartman said.

Drake ignored Hartman and approached the medical examiner, who stood up and acknowledged him. "What do you know?" Drake asked.

"What's to know? My partner's dead." Hartman grabbed Drake by the arm. "I'm not going to ask again. What are you doing here?"

Drake looked down at his arm where Hartman held him, then he looked up into Hartman's stern gaze. Drake, his jaw muscles twitching, won the stare-off, and Hartman released his grip. "I heard it called in on the police band, and I came right over."

"It wasn't called in," Hartman said. "We were tipped off by an anonymous note left at the station. We've kept it quiet so far."

Drake said nothing.

"Who tipped you off?" Hartman asked.

"Why don't you just tell me what happened."

"Why don't you get the fuck out of here while you can still walk."

Drake kept his eyes locked on Hartman, unflinching, then he turned to the medical examiner, hoping for something, but he wasn't in a sharing mood. Drake realized he was wasting his time, and he walked away, made it about ten feet.

"Where were you last night?" Hartman asked.

Drake took one step in Hartman's direction, and he stopped and glared at Hartman with an expression that conveyed the situation might just get violent. Hartman wasn't likely intimidated, since he had the manpower and firepower to subdue Drake without much effort. Drake lit a cigarette and stared at Hartman. He waited a moment then turned and walked back across the deserted marina parking lot and headed toward home.

18

Back at his apartment, Drake started to come unhinged, his mind and body reacting in a way he had not experienced in a long time, not since that fateful day, years ago, when his assignment with the Agency had gone horribly wrong. He sat at his desk in his dark apartment, drinking and smoking and trying to squelch the smoldering ember of rage in his gut. A dull headache loomed behind his eyes as he tried desperately to make sense of Angie's death.

It was clear to Drake that Angie was more than a one-night stand, that he had developed feelings for her, new feelings but familiar, like those he had felt with Karen when they first met. Images and memories flashed in quick succession through his mind like an old slide projector: his first meeting with Angie at the police station; Angie sitting across from him at the bar, smiling; the two of them in his apartment, Angie rubbing against him and their passionate kiss; Drake looking at her angelic face while she slept in his bed; Angie in the morning, standing in the doorway of his bedroom, wide-eyed and enticing him to come back to bed.

Drake emptied his glass and refilled it. While one cigarette

was still lit in the ashtray, he lit another and drew on it hard.
He inhaled, closed his eyes, and blew the smoke up toward
the ceiling. A dense cloud hung in the air, thick and pungent.
Perspiration glistened on his forehead. He opened his eyes
and stared into the depths of the darkened room.

He looked down at the top of his desk, at the portfolio
Engel had given to him.

More images and memories flashed in his mind, this time
in black and white, like a high-speed silent picture show: in his
apartment and at his desk, sitting across from Engel at their
first meeting; walking through Engel's mansion; his phone
call with Engel last night; his phone call with him today.

Drake was racking his brain, trying to piece it all
together, feeling there might be a connection. *There had to
be a connection.* But no answer came to him. He rubbed his
temples in an effort to subdue the now piercing pain there.

He was distracted by a heavy knock at the door.

"Drake, it's Hartman. Open the door."

Drake did not respond and remained at his desk. He
downed his glass of bourbon once more and refilled it. He
smoked and struggled with his thoughts and feelings, his
loss. He had not spent much time with Angie but felt he had
made a connection, that there was something developing
between them, a real relationship. And now it was gone,
over, ended. His stomach ached, and he felt empty inside,
the same way he felt the day he signed his divorce papers.

"I know you're in there. Open the door."

Again, Drake did not respond.

After a silent moment, just long enough that Drake
thought Hartman might have given up and left, the doorjamb

splintered, the door swung open fast and hit hard against the wall, and Hartman barged into the apartment. Two uniformed police officers followed him in.

Drake looked at Hartman. "That was unnecessary."

"Get up," Hartman said.

Drake remained seated.

Any patience Hartman might have had before his arrival dissipated. He looked around, struggled with the darkness, then leaned over Drake's desk and turned on the lamp. To the officers he said, "Search the place."

"What are you doing? Do you have a warrant?"

"Fuck you," Hartman said, waving a document. "You know, it's funny. I don't see you for years, and then you magically appear. In the matter of a couple of days, you're walking around the station like you're some big time investigator, like you own the place. You're a fucking writer, and a shitty one at that. To make matters worse, you're causing trouble for the most powerful family in the state and bringing a world of shit down on the chief. And then my partner . . ." He grunted, and his face twitched as he tried to hold back his emotions.

"You think I'm responsible?" Drake asked.

One of the officers was over by the couch. He had Drake's jacket in one hand, a set of keys in the other. "Detective Hartman?"

Hartman turned.

"You might want to look at these," the officer said as he shook the keys.

Hartman walked over, grabbed the keys, and inspected them. "You've got some explaining to do, you son of a bitch."

He pulled the Glock pistol from his belt holster and pointed it at Drake. "We can make this easy or very, very difficult."

Drake ignored him. He downed his drink and lit another cigarette.

"Get up. We're going to the station."

"What are you talking about?"

While still pointing the gun and holding up the keys, Hartman said, "These are the keys to Angie's car, which happens to be parked out in front of your building. What happened? She came here last night, you tried to move on her, and she resisted . . . and then you killed her?"

Drake shook his head, couldn't believe the nonsense.

Hartman said to the officers, "Cuff him."

As the police officers approached Drake, he stood up, and they reacted, putting hands on guns and itching to draw them. Drake thought they appeared much too excited, just hoping for a reason to pull the trigger, so he raised his hands, palms out in submission, then turned around and joined them behind his neck. The police officers approached with caution, then they pounced on him with brute aggression, forced him facedown hard onto the desk, and cuffed him. Each officer had Drake by an arm, and they walked him toward Hartman.

Drake planted his feet, forcing the officers to stop. "Hartman, you're not a good detective."

"You have the right to shut the fuck up," Hartman said. He looked around, appeared he was not impressed with the surroundings. His mouth twitched, as if he had tasted something foul, then he spit on the hardwood floor at Drake's feet. "Get him out of here."

The police officers led Drake out of the apartment, and Hartman followed them, leaving the broken door open wide.

* * *

Drake sat in a quiet and empty interrogation room at the 18th District Police Station: worn linoleum, three blank walls painted a shade of dust, one wall with the requisite two-way mirror, metal furniture from a past decade, and harsh lighting. The room smelled of sweat, the air stale. He was mentally unraveling a little more, losing his edge it seemed, smoking like a fiend and having difficulty grasping what had transpired over the last day and the reality of Angie's murder. Further, he wondered about how his life had been flipped upside down all in just a few days. In the past, when he was younger, he was able to deal with drastic changes and stressful situations, but that was a long time ago, before his last job with the Agency. He sat still, unemotional, and became more ragged as the minutes passed.

The door of the room opened, and Hartman walked in, still pissed off and appearing determined to get answers. He saw Drake smoking and was instantly annoyed. "You can't smoke in here."

Drake took a long drag and inhaled hard. He looked at the cigarette as smoke streamed from his nostrils, then he searched the room for somewhere to put it.

"Just put it out," Hartman said. "Fucking loser."

Drake dropped the cigarette to the floor and snubbed it out with his shoe. He looked at his watch. "It's been three hours. Giving me time to think about what I did?" His sarcasm was palpable.

"Where were you last night?"

"I'd like to make a phone call."

Hartman shook his head. "What's the matter with you? You think you're living in a dream world? Where were you?"

True to form, Drake did not respond.

Hartman looked over toward the two-way mirror.

Drake asked, "Who's on the other side, the good cop?"

Hartman shook his head again, exhaled as though he was blowing out a candle, and took a moment to suppress his already evident frustration, all while still looking at the two-way mirror. Then he conceded, and he pulled a phone out of his pocket and tossed it to Drake.

Drake saw that it was *his* phone. "I was looking for this." He dialed a call and listened.

Thomas Engel answered the call. "Hello, Mr. Drake. What can I do for you?"

"I'm at the police station, the 18th. They think I had something to do with Angie Parker's murder."

"Have you been charged?"

"No."

"Do not say anything. I will be there in fifteen minutes."

"Can you do me a favor?" Drake asked.

"Of course."

"Call Ray Parsons, the State's Attorney, and let him know that I'm here."

Engel said, "Are you sure that is wise? I can offer you another alternative."

"Just call him."

"Very well."

Drake ended the call. As he was about to put the phone

into his pocket, Hartman reacted and reached out his hand. "I'll take that."

Drake slid the phone across the table.

Hartman grabbed it before it fell off the edge and put it in his pocket. "I'm only going to ask you one more time. Where were you last night?"

"I was in my apartment."

"Were you with anyone?"

"I was alone."

"Can anyone corroborate your story?"

"No."

Hartman didn't believe him. "You were having a relation-ship with Angie."

Drake shook his head. "Believe what you want."

"She told me. We were partners. She told me everything."

"I don't think so."

"Did you kill her?"

"No," Drake said. "You know I'm not involved."

Hartman appeared to accept the answer. He looked over at the mirror. He paused, thinking, then asked, "How did you get her car keys?"

"They were in my mailbox when I checked for the mail this morning."

"There's no mail delivery on Sunday."

"I didn't get around to it yesterday."

"Yeah, sure."

Drake shrugged and wished he could fire up another cigarette. He reached into his pocket and felt the pack. Knowing they were close seemed to satisfy him.

Hartman said, "I found out Angie was working on the

Mitchell case. The chief had told us to stay away, but she was going after it hard for some reason, on her own time. Did she talk to you about anything?"

"No."

Hartman paced back and forth, his hands in his pockets, and nibbled on his bottom lip. There was a yellow legal pad and pen on the table. Hartman leaned down and slid them over to Drake. "Why don't you write down everything you've done for the last five days, and I mean everything. You have the time, so be as detailed as you wish. I want to know where you've been, what you've done, who you were with. I even want to know where you took your last piss."

"That's a bit personal."

"Don't push me," Hartman said. He left the room and slammed the door behind him.

Drake grabbed the pen and stared down at the blank sheet. He thought for a moment, then wrote something down, drew a box around it, and filled in the rest of the page with some elaborate doodles to pass the time. When he was done, he set the pen down and stared at the box he had drawn.

On the page, inside the box, was the single word: JERRY.

19

Early in the evening, a couple of hours past quitting time, Police Chief Peters was in his office at the 18th and behind his desk, stewing. He was not having a good day. Cook County State's Attorney Ray Parsons sat across from him. The chief had a dead detective on his hands and a suspect in custody, and he would not be leaving until he was comfortable with the department's approach to the investigation. The chief was hoping to keep a lid on the situation until he had something more solid, but Parsons had just shown up a few minutes earlier, unannounced, and wanted to talk about the Parker murder and the man they had in custody. The chief had planned to call Parsons after Hartman interrogated Drake, and he wondered how the word had leaked, how Parsons had been notified.

Hartman stepped into the office doorway and knocked on the doorframe. "You wanted to see me, Chief?"

The chief looked up. "Mike, you know State's Attorney Parsons."

Parsons stood up from his chair, and Hartman stepped into the office. They shook hands.

"Of course," Hartman said.

Parsons sat. Hartman remained standing.

The chief said, "Mr. Parsons stopped by, and I filled him in on the Parker case."

"I'm very sorry about your partner," Parsons said.

"Thanks," Hartman said.

The chief said to Hartman, "Do we have anything on Mr. Drake?"

"I'm still interrogating him."

"What has he said?" Parsons asked.

Hartman looked at the chief, who nodded. "My partner's car was found parked outside of Mr. Drake's apartment. *He* had the keys. He said he found them in the mailbox. How convenient. Said he was alone in his apartment last night, but there's no one to corroborate."

"Anything else?" the chief asked.

"I think he was having a relationship with her."

"Any proof?" Parsons asked.

"No."

"Any other leads?"

"Not yet. We should have the medical examiner's report by the end of the day. Maybe that will give us something."

The chief asked, "Anything else, on Drake?"

"Like I said, I'm still interrogating."

Chief Peters and Parsons looked at each other. Chief Peters shook his head. "Let him go."

"What?" Hartman said, flabbergasted.

"He's not going anywhere," the chief said. "We know where he lives. And he still needs our help on the Mitchell case."

"But—"

"Mike, let him go."

"Unbelievable," Hartman said, and he left the chief's office, pounding on the doorframe as he passed it.

Parsons asked, "The Mitchell case?"

"Sarah Mitchell, daughter of the senator, severed hand left in the park, ten years ago. The body was never recovered."

"No, no, I know the case. It's been cold for eight years. What's he doing?"

"He's been hired by a private citizen to review the evidence. There's nothing there. He won't find anything."

Parsons expressed concern. "We don't need any publicity rising up about that case."

"I realize that," the chief said. "We're keeping a close eye on him and his investigation."

"Don't forget what happened last time."

"You don't need to remind me. I'm the one who was almost ruined."

Parsons stood up and reached over the desk to shake hands. "Chief."

The chief stood and shook his hand. "Ray."

Parsons left the office. Chief Peters put his hands into his pants pockets and watched Parsons walk down the hall. He stood firm, analyzing his current predicament.

* * *

After Drake had spent another unnecessary hour sitting and waiting in the locked interrogation room, Hartman came in and told him, reluctantly, that he could leave. As Drake stood, Hartman was right in his face. "Don't leave the country, or the city for that matter."

"Where would I go?" Drake asked, locking eyes with Hartman. Uncomfortable seconds passed before Hartman stepped aside so Drake could pass. "Get a mint," Drake said, and he walked out of the interrogation room and down the hall.

Drake exited the front entrance of the police station and saw Engel standing on the steps, waiting for him. Same coat, same hat, same umbrella. Drake took out a cigarette and lit it.

"Good evening, Mr. Drake," Engel said as Drake approached him. "I trust they were cordial and accommodating during your stay?"

"Yeah, sure."

"It appears Mr. Parsons was helpful?"

"It appears so."

"How did you come to know of him?"

"We crossed paths once or twice," Drake said.

Engel reached into his breast pocket and pulled out an envelope, which he handed to Drake. "I look forward to working with you for another week."

Drake took the envelope and slipped it into his jacket pocket.

"Mr. Drake. I would like to add a benefit to your employment agreement."

"I don't need health care."

"I was thinking of something more practical. You need a car." Engel pulled a set of keys from his pocket and handed them to Drake. "We still have quite a bit of work to do, and a taxi will not suffice. I took the liberty of selecting a car for you. I hope you find it suitable."

Engel waved a hand toward the street, where a 1967 Mercury Cougar XR7 was parked.

"A '67 Cougar. Nice," Drake said. "Yours?"

"One of my favorites, but it has been sitting too long. It needs some air, some exercise. Will it be sufficient?"

"It will do." Drake actually knew the car well. Back as a teenager in his old Andersonville neighborhood, one of the older guys, Jeff Cooper, had a 1968 Cougar in powder blue, and since that time, Drake had been an admirer of classic late-sixties cars, the Cougar in particular. The Cougar was Mercury's answer to the Ford Mustang, was pitched as more of a gentleman's muscle car, and Drake had always preferred its more unknown and understated design. Engel's car was a deep shade of maroon, a color that looked like dried blood in the shadow of the streetlights, and it had a black vinyl top, which was now an outdated option but Drake thought it fit the car well. *Of all the possibilities, he brings me a Cougar.*

Ray Parsons exited the building. He descended the stairs and stopped alongside Drake and Engel. He said to Drake, "The Mitchell case, huh?"

Drake said, "Ray Parsons, this is Thomas Engel. His brother was engaged to Sarah Mitchell. He's not convinced the case should be closed."

Parsons shook hands with Engel. "Mr. Engel."

"Mr. Parsons," Engel said.

"Thanks for your help tonight," Drake said to Parsons. "I appreciate it."

"No problem, but tell me, Drake, how do *you* fit in all this?"

"I had some free time," Drake said, "and Mr. Engel thought I could help."

"A little investigative journalism? Like the old days?" Parsons asked.

"You could say that."

Parsons considered the situation. "You do understand that the Mitchell family is quite powerful in this state, in this city."

"I do."

It was clear that Parsons was trying to make sense of why Drake might be involved in the Mitchell case, a closed and very cold case. Drake hoped he would lose interest.

Engel kept quiet.

"Drake, might I ask a favor?" Parsons asked.

"Why not."

"If you find anything, anything at all, you'll let me know before you say or do anything?"

Drake looked at Engel, who nodded.

"Sure," Drake said. He had made a similar promise to Chief Peters, but that did not concern him.

Parsons seemed relieved. "Well, then, have a good evening." He looked at Engel suspiciously. "Mr. Engel."

Engel kept his hands folded in front of him. He bowed his head. "Mr. Parsons."

Parsons descended the stairs and headed down the street. Drake and Engel watched him for a moment, not saying anything, then Drake descended the stairs and slid into his newly acquired employee benefit. He started up the car, listened to the throaty rumble of the engine, and put it into gear. He pulled away from the curb, confident and with authority, and took the opportunity to screech the tires and leave some rubber on the street.

* * *

After Drake had left, Hartman walked back into the empty interrogation room. He saw the snubbed-out cigarette on the floor then noticed the yellow legal pad on the table and walked over to it. He spun the pad around to see what Drake had written. Most of the top part of the page was filled with nonsense—scribbles and childish doodles as though from a fifth grader—but in the middle of the sheet and enclosed within a thick-lined box, he saw: JERRY.

Hartman stared at the pad, at the name. "Jerry," he said aloud.

He turned back toward the door, replaying in his mind the moment earlier when Drake walked out. *What the hell is he up to?*

20

Drake appreciated the Cougar; it made him happy, if only a little, and temporarily took his mind off the troubles of the day. It was a fine car: classic, mint condition, engine power like a rocket, and responsive handling. The interior of the car appeared restored to its original condition, at least visually, but Drake noticed a number of modifications that Engel had incorporated for pure driver comfort. The black leather of the bucket seats was soft and inviting, and the cabin was quiet, dead quiet, the result of what had to be a painstaking effort of installing soundproofing material and replacing the seals between every opening and gap to the outside world and the engine compartment. It was a pleasure to drive, and he wondered why automakers didn't just go back and build the classic cars of the fifties, sixties, and early seventies. Many of those cars had proven successful, and there were a record number of baby boomers wishing they could drive the cars of their youth.

Drake was back at his apartment at eight that evening. He had made a couple of stops on the way, and he walked through the still-open front door carrying a pizza and a six-pack of beer. He closed the door and was surprised to see that it stayed closed with no doorjamb or locking mechanism in place. He took off his coat then grabbed a slice of pizza and a beer, went over to his desk, and sat down. He was tired and took a moment to reflect on the hellish day.

He awakened the computer on his desk, and there again in front of him was the first page of his new novel. The story was there in his mind and had been for some time, but now there were a substantial number of pages that made the story real. Now there was a purpose, to flesh out the story and uncover how it would end, and the story was leading him along, taking control of him, as it did in the past when he was able to write. He took a bite of pizza and leaned back in the chair, looking at the screen, staring at the title page.

A FINE LINE
A Jack Cannon Novel
By Sebastian Drake

The sight of the title calmed him. He leaned forward and scrolled down through the document, savoring the accomplishment in each page. It was evident that he had broken through his writer's block and that his past few days had been productive. He scrolled down to a blank page and started to type.

Cannon had only been on the trail for a few days, yet the trail was getting messy, blurring fast. Each question he asked had spawned five others, and each person he talked to became a character beyond belief.

There's no way I could make up characters like these, Cannon had thought.

The case file was too neat, too perfect. It seemed everyone had a secret. With each new day, more characters were being added to the story, and they had secrets as well. If he were to have any chance at all of solving the case, it was clear to Cannon that he would have to open the door to his past. He would need the special skills hidden there to deal with these people.

He walked over to the bookcase and when he pushed gently at the top right corner of the frame, the bookcase slid out and sideways to reveal a safe. He spun the dial forward and back and forward again. Then he raised the lever, which retracted steel bolts, and opened the safe door. He pulled out a wooden box, which he put under his arm, then reached in and pulled out a bottle of bourbon. He looked at the label, was wistful, and felt his whole body relax.

Drake stopped typing. He looked over at the bottle of bourbon on his desk.

On his way to the sofa, Cannon grabbed a rocks glass from the cabinet. He sat down on the sofa and set the box and the bottle before him, positioned them just right, ceremoniously. He opened the bottle and poured three fingers worth into the glass, then he lifted the glass and stared at it in wonder. It had been three years since his last drink, a lifetime ago for a man with an insatiable craving for alcohol, but it did not seem that long ago. It was time to say "hello" to an old friend, and no one would be the wiser.

Drake stopped again and poured himself a glass of bourbon. He typed.

> *Cannon took the glass and downed it fast and in one motion. The bourbon created a once-again memorable burn as it rinsed his tonsils. He said to the glass, "Hello, friend."*

Drake picked up his glass and downed it, savoring the taste as the liquid heated his throat and chest like he had gulped a cup of steaming milk. He set the glass down and resumed typing.

> *Cannon set the glass down then opened the box. He looked down at his other old friend, away three years as well. This friend was an original World War II-era Colt 1911, a pistol known for its .45-caliber stopping power and reliability, a gift given to him by his father before he died. A gift from a man who fought for the same cause, for the same agency that his son once fought for—an agency that seldom allowed participation from the next generation. Cannon picked up the gun and held it, feeling the weight of it in his hands and in his memories.*
>
> *Cannon had gone to great lengths over the years to keep his history with the agency a secret—in the past, where it belonged. His new employer had somehow dug it all up again and felt his past experience would prove helpful to the case and the investigation. The line between his past and the present was becoming thin, very thin. It was a fine line, and Cannon was walking the line like a*

journeyman high-wire walker. Only now he could see the faint outline of a person kneeling down at the end of the line, working at the metal cable with a wire cutter.

Drake leaned back and stared at the page. He reached for the bottle, poured himself another drink, and downed it. He poured another then lit a cigarette and smoked while he stared at the screen and mouthed the words he had just written.

He emptied his glass once again and leaned forward to attack the keys. He continued typing, long into the night.

* * *

At nine o'clock the following morning, Drake was still lying in his bed, sleeping. He had had a long night. In time, the harsh, morning light came in through the bedroom windows and splashed across his face. He woke up, opened his eyelids just a crack, then squeezed them closed tight and covered his eyes with an arm. Dreams still covered his brain like a heavy blanket. His entire body felt sore, as if he had taken a severe beating during the night, and he tried not to move. He licked his dry lips and attempted to moisten the desert in his mouth. It was no use. He sat up, groaned, and rubbed his face and eyes. He was bewildered and hoping to clear the haze in his sight.

He grabbed his watch from the nightstand, squinted to read the time, and realized that he had lost a good portion of the morning already. He sighed. After such a fruitful evening of writing, he felt the day was now getting away from him. He swung his feet over the edge of the bed and stood up quickly—too quickly—and was unprepared for the hot wave of darkness that dashed across his eyes. He set his feet and, as a reflex, waved at the air. He took a deep breath and steadied himself. *I have to quit drinking.*

In his T-shirt and boxers, he walked through the bedroom doorway, into the kitchen area, and straight to the coffee maker. He pulled out the carafe, which was filled with day-old coffee, then searched for a mug. On the counter, he found one—maybe a day old, maybe more, and used—which he held up and inspected. Nothing moved inside it, so it would do. He poured himself a cupful of the old coffee then looked at the microwave. The thought of heating the coffee passed, and he took a sip of the cold coffee and grimaced.

He made it over to his desk and sat down. The chair was still warm from the previous evening, and his forehead felt warm to his touch. He had a headache pulsing behind his eyes and an unsettling emptiness growing in his stomach, and he could imagine he looked just as bad as he felt. He lit a cigarette, took a short drag, and inhaled lightly, not wanting to exacerbate his raw throat. He took another sip of coffee, grimaced again, and wished he had started a fresh pot. He poured a little bourbon into the cup and took another sip. He didn't need the bourbon, but the coffee did.

He awakened his computer again and settled down to work on his book. As if by instinct, he began where he left off and typed a flurry of words in a three-minute burst, then he stopped. A flash of a thought had interrupted him: *Angie.* He closed his eyes, massaged his skull, and rubbed his face and eyes again, covering them with his hands to shield him from the room.

The familiar series of images that spanned his short-lived relationship with her flashed through his mind: his first meeting with Angie at the police station; Angie sitting across from him at the bar, smiling; the two of them in his apartment, Angie rubbing against him, and their passionate kiss; Drake looking at her angelic face while she slept in his bed; Angie in the morning, standing in the doorway of his bedroom, wide-eyed and enticing him to come back to bed. The sequence of images repeated, time and again, faster and faster then faster still, like a movie projector gone wild.

"Stop!"

He dropped his hands from his face and opened his eyes. The apartment was quiet and still, but he felt the room and its contents passing judgment on him. His heartbeat pounded in his ears.

Drake sat at the desk, paralyzed, emotionally and physically, both from the hangover and impact of Angie's death, more so because of Angie. He felt responsible. He felt his entire being degrade and dissolve as the seconds passed, as though he was stuck in the top section of an hourglass, squeezing into and falling through the opening and down into a disjointed mess below, grain by grain. He stood up, shuffled back into the bedroom, and fell face forward down onto the bed, where he lay, motionless.

* * *

The phone in Drake's bedroom rang. After five rings, the

answering machine switched on and played Drake's recorded greeting. The machine beeped.

"Sebastian, it's Karen. Pick up, it's an emergency."

Drake was still lying on the bed, unmoving.

"Sebastian, please, pick up the phone," Karen said, louder and frantic.

Drake opened one eye and processed the words.

"Sebastian!"

He bolted upright and reached for the phone on the nightstand. He grabbed the handset, fumbled it, and put it to his ear. He shook his head, tried to clear the fog in his mind. "What, what is it?"

"It's Samantha. She's gone."

"What?"

In clipped words, Karen said, "The school called. She never made it there this morning. Her friend, Ashley—who she walks with—made it to school, hysterical, saying that Samantha was kidnapped. A black van pulled up alongside them. Two big men grabbed her and drove away."

Drake put the words together, tried to make sense of them. *Samantha . . . black van . . . two big men.* "I don't under—"

"Sebastian, she's been kidnapped!"

"I, I don't, I don't know . . ." It seemed his sanity was slipping away, and he felt like he was in a dream.

"Sebastian, I need you. You have to find her."

Drake covered his eyes with one hand. His mind raced. His pulse quickened.

"The police have been notified," Karen said, "and the school is doing all they can. Ted is driving around the neighborhood, searching."

Drake found no words, could say nothing.

Karen seemed to calm some as she said, "*Sebastian.*"

"Yeah."

"They took our baby."

"Yeah. I'm on it."

Drake hung up the phone. He looked at the clock on the nightstand. It showed 9:30. He lay back down and stared at the ceiling with blazing, wild eyes. His face felt flushed, and a film of heavy perspiration rose on his forehead. He felt like he was on the edge of reality, teetering back and forth between the past and the here-and-now, walking a fine line between good and evil . . . and falling, diving, and spiraling out of control.

The feeling Drake was experiencing was familiar, a nervous breakdown of a sort, and it came about and evolved in the same manner as when everything fell apart after his second and final assignment with the Agency. It was the only way his body and mind knew how to deal with such a situation, one where his work had not proceeded as planned and he was thrown into a pressure cooker of a predicament.

A situation where an innocent human life was jeopardized.

21

Almost two hours had passed since Karen's call, and Drake was still lying on the bed with the same wild eyes, staring at the ceiling, held in the vice grip of a total physical and mental shutdown. He hadn't moved. The room was cold and silent. His T-shirt was soaked.

There was a loud knock on the door of the apartment.

He didn't move, couldn't move.

"Drake, open up," Scotty said in a loud, booming voice. "It's Scotty."

He heard the door open and close, footsteps coming toward the bedroom. He turned his head toward the doorway and saw Scotty standing there.

"Drake," Scotty said, surprised to see him lying on the bed. He walked to the foot of the bed and shook Drake's foot.

He blinked and snapped out of his daze.

"Drake, are you all right?"

Drake shook his head again, tried to clear the cobwebs floating in his eyes, and rubbed his temples.

"What's going on? I left you three messages yesterday. Then, this morning, I received a call from Karen. She told me about Samantha."

Drake sat up in the bed, was gradually returning to reality.

"I don't need to tell you that some disturbing things have happened since you started working on the Mitchell case. It's all too much to be a coincidence."

Drake looked up at Scotty with a blank expression, searching his face for an answer, trying to fit puzzle pieces together in his mind.

"Listen, Drake, you need to get yourself together. Don't worry about your family right now."

Drake stared at Scotty, couldn't believe what he had said. "What?"

"I called in a favor. The Agency will have nothing to do with it, but some of our old friends are more than happy to get involved, for old times' sake. There's a team covering your house, and another is shadowing the local authorities to search for Samantha."

"I need to find her," Drake said.

"No, you need to come with me."

"What—what are you talking about?"

"You asked me to look into this guy, Jerry. The name you gave me. His name is Jerry Fitzsimmons. He was Senator Mitchell's advisor, always in the shadows and out of the media, and he is a close, very close, personal friend."

Drake wasn't following.

"We need to go visit him, to find out what he knows. Now. Get some clothes on."

Drake searched the room then decided to go the easy route. He crawled out of bed, picked up his jeans from the floor, and put them on.

Scotty said, "Like I said—Detective Parker, Samantha—it's not a coincidence."

"How do you know about Angie?" Drake asked.

"Come on. You really think I'd let you do this job on your own? We're a team, remember, and you involved me when you showed me the bullets Engel gave you."

Drake took comfort, was relieved some in knowing Scotty was involved and there to help him.

"I think you've opened a can of worms here, my friend, a chapter of history that someone would prefer stays closed and in the past."

Drake nodded.

"It's time to finish the job, Drake."

"Yeah."

"If we find out who killed Detective Parker," Scotty said, "I think we'll find the person who has your daughter . . . and likely a person who was involved in the murder of Sarah Mitchell."

Drake reached into the loops of his shoulder holster and pulled it down over his T-shirt then grabbed a black blazer and put it on. He ran his hands through his hair in a feeble attempt at grooming. "Give me a minute," he said as he ducked into the bathroom.

Scotty walked into the living room.

A minute later, Drake came out of the bedroom, towel in hand, wiping his face and hair. He seemed to have shaken his demon, even if only temporarily, and he had his edge back.

Scotty was standing by the door, waiting for him.

"Let's go," Drake said.

They left the apartment, Drake closing the busted door behind them.

* * *

Drake and Scotty took the Cougar and drove over to the Gold Coast area, just north of downtown and west of Lake Shore Drive. From his online Agency resources, Scotty had obtained Jerry Fitzsimmons' address on east Cedar Street. After a fifteen-minute drive, which took them east and then north on Michigan Avenue and past Oak Street Beach, they turned left onto Cedar then proceeded a half block down and pulled up in front of Mr. Fitzsimmons' residence. Drake shifted the car into park, leaned forward, and looked past Scotty to survey the house.

He was familiar with the neighborhood, having visited Thomas Engel just days before, a few blocks away. This block was different, though, as the properties were not quite on par with those on Engel's street, but it was still a desirable and expensive location. Fitzsimmons lived in a 1920s greystone: narrow but tall, three stories, with masonry steps and railings that led up through a stone archway to a covered porch, a small balcony above, a pitched roof covered with clay tiles, and copper gutters.

"What does he do for a living now?" Drake asked. Properties on the street were pricey. Fitzsimmons' house was worth two million, he figured, and he wondered about Fitzsimmons' wealth and how he might have acquired it.

"The Agency file on him was slight. It was clear, however, that he was a problem solver. If Senator Mitchell had an issue, Mr. Fitzsimmons made it go away."

"A *cleaner*," Drake said.

"That's right."

Drake took his pistol from its holster. He ejected and checked the magazine: eight bullets, *his* bullets, the ones from Engel. He reinserted the magazine and pulled back then released the slide, loading a round into the chamber. He put the gun back into its holster.

Scotty asked, "Why would Senator Mitchell tell you about Fitzsimmons?"

"I'm not sure he meant to or realized it. Maybe it's the Alzheimer's . . . or the medication. Who knows?" Drake opened his door. "Let's go talk to Mr. Fitzsimmons."

They stepped out of the car, walked up the front steps, and stopped at the front door.

Scotty rang the doorbell. "Fitzsimmons is an old, crafty, and squirrelly man. He's sixty, but in the images on file, he looks much older. He knows how to play the game of politics and wades easily in a sea of filth and corruption. He's experienced and feels privileged. Always did what he was told and always got what he wanted, but in the end, he's just a high-society wannabe who never quite had what it takes. In the file images, he's always grinning, like a cat who just ate a mouse."

"Interesting."

"I'd say he's the devil's apprentice," Scotty said.

The door opened. Before them stood an older man, thin and gaunt, almost sickly looking. The man said, "Mr. Drake, I presume."

Drake and Scotty looked at each other, surprised.

Drake asked, "Mr. Fitzsimmons, Jerry Fitzsimmons?"

"Yes, yes, that's me. Why don't you come in?"

He held the door open for Drake and Scotty, and they entered the foyer.

Fitzsimmons asked Scotty, "And you are?"

"You were expecting me?" Drake asked.

"I was made aware of your involvement in the Sarah Mitchell case," Fitzsimmons said. "I figured it was just a matter of time until you showed up on my doorstep."

"Who made you aware?"

"May I take your coats, gentlemen?"

Drake and Scotty declined his offer by ignoring his question.

Drake looked around at the elaborate and detailed woodwork, the marble floor, the solid walnut wainscoting that rose halfway up to the fourteen-foot ceiling, the gilded crown moldings, and a small but elegant crystal chandelier.

"Nice place."

"Why, thank you."

"Are you the caretaker?" Scotty asked.

"Excuse me?"

"Your house is owned by a trust, which happens to be controlled by the Mitchell family. Did they hire you to look after it?"

"I see you've done your homework, Mr.—"

Scotty ignored him.

Fitzsimmons laughed, appeared nervous. "I can assure you that this is my home, that I own it, and that I've earned the home and everything in it." He looked at them and forced a smile. "Why don't we go into the library?" He turned around and shuffled away.

Fitzsimmons walked down the hall and into the library. Drake and Scotty were close behind. He sat down in a wingback chair and waved a hand. "Gentlemen, please, sit down and make yourselves comfortable." He reached for a cigarette on the lamp table, put it into his mouth, and lit it.

Drake and Scotty, again, declined his offer and remained standing just inside the room.

"Mr. Fitzsimmons, do you still work for the Mitchell family?" Drake asked.

"I'm retired, have been for some time now."

"The family employed you at the time that Sarah Mitchell was murdered?"

"They did." He drew on his cigarette and considered his next words, sucked his teeth, then dug a fingernail in between his two front ones. He looked at his fingernail, saw something that likely remained from breakfast, and licked it off. "It was a terrible time. Miss Sarah, so young and gifted. She was a piano prodigy ready to embark on a meteoric musical career. Her life cut short by a madman."

"Why is it that you were not interviewed in connection with her murder?"

"What do you mean?"

"I've reviewed all of the records," Drake said. "Everything. Your name doesn't appear once."

Fitzsimmons thought about Drake's statement while he continued to smoke.

"Why is that?"

"It's very simple, Mr. Drake. I was a business employee of Senator Mitchell, that's all, one of hundreds. I had nothing to do with the family or their personal affairs."

"Do you know Billy Taylor?"

"I do. He was a close friend of the fam—" Fitzsimmons caught himself.

"Billy and I had a chance to talk," Drake said. "It seems he was close to the family and was especially close to Sarah."

"You know he's mentally challenged, right?"

"He implied that Alderman Mitchell might have been involved somehow."

"That's ludicrous." Fitzsimmons snorted, and his face showed a glint of agitation.

Drake noticed and grinned.

Fitzsimmons said, "The boy is retarded, clueless."

"It's what he said."

"Mr. Drake, it's clear to me that you're fishing. I understand Mr. Engel's desire—yes, I know all about Mr. Engel. I understand his desire to, once and for all, find Sarah's killer and put the case to rest. We all *had* that same desire. And I know all about you, Mr. Drake, and I know that your past life as an investigative reporter for the *Chicago Tribune* does not provide you with the skills necessary to solve this particular mystery. You're not that good."

"I'm pretty good," Drake said. "Does Billy know *you*?"

Fitzsimmons pursed his lips and twitched. "Mr. Drake, the case, unfortunately, is closed. We have all put it behind us. I suggest you do the same."

Drake thought for a moment. "If you insist," he said then turned to leave.

"That's it?" Scotty asked.

"It's time to go." Drake walked to the doorway, and Scotty followed him.

"I heard you were a smart man," Fitzsimmons said.

Drake stopped. He looked at the credenza that lined the near wall. It was a grand piece of furniture that looked like it was carved from a single piece of wood. The drawers were almost unnoticeable because of their perfect fit and were adorned with antiqued brass hardware. The short legs were carved and ornate, and the entire surface had a polished, glossy finish. On top of the credenza was a crystal vase, round with a bell-shaped mouth and filled with a unique flower arrangement.

"That's an interesting flower," Drake said.

"Mr. Drake, an appreciation for flowers? I never would have thought."

Drake turned around to face Fitzsimmons. "I enjoy them as much as the next guy."

"You have good taste. They are vanilla orchids."

Drake acknowledged the statement with a nod. "We'll let ourselves out." They left the room and walked down the hall toward the foyer.

Fitzsimmons had watched them leave and had remained seated. Now, with a raised voice, Fitzsimmons said, "It was a pleasure, Mr. Drake. Come back again sometime."

Drake and Scotty paid no attention to him, walked out through the front door, and stood for a moment on the front landing.

"That's it?" Scotty asked again, surprised that Drake had given up so easily.

"For now," Drake said. "Did you notice his reaction when I mentioned Billy?"

"No."

"I have a hunch. Let's go see Billy."

They descended the stairs, hurried to the car, and sped away.

22

Drake and Scotty raced back over to the South Side. Drake felt the clock ticking, that time was getting away from him, and he was no closer to finding his daughter. As he drove, he questioned his decision to leave the search for his daughter to the authorities, but Scotty was right—there was likely a connection between the disappearance of his daughter and his involvement in the Mitchell case. He had to be out looking in places where others were not, into situations no one else was even considering. It was the only way to get his daughter back safely.

Based on Fitzsimmons' reaction, Drake also had a feeling that the clock was ticking for Billy Taylor.

Billy lived in the same Bridgeport neighborhood as the grocery store where he worked, and as a result of Drake's recent visit to the store, his route was familiar: the straight route south on Archer Avenue to Ashland, then south on Ashland, left on West 33rd Street, and right on Justine Street. They approached a ramshackle small, aluminum-sided ranch on a dead-end side street in a neighborhood of well-maintained homes. With a hanging gutter and a lawn comprised mostly of dirt, Billy's house stood out from the rest. Parked cars lined the street in both directions. There was one open space, and Drake pulled in.

They exited the car and walked up to the house. As they climbed the steps, they noticed that the door was ajar. They looked at each other and silently agreed on protocol. Drake stepped forward and listened through the opening. He gently pushed the door open and entered. Scotty followed him in.

They entered a small empty foyer and stood on opposite sides of the archway that led to the living room, their backs against the wall, out of sight. Drake peered into the room and saw two men, each with linebacker proportions, sufficient hair grease, and a lot of pent-up aggression, beating Billy to a pulp and taunting him as though they were schoolyard bullies. Billy was on the floor, cowering and pleading with them to stop. The two thugs paid no attention and were kicking him in the head, stomach, and back with reckless abandon. They acted as if they were having fun.

Drake stepped into the room. "Excuse me. We're from the cable company. The door was open."

One of the thugs looked up, surprised and annoyed. "Get lost."

The other one turned, seemed to recognize Drake, and grinned. "We were going to visit you next. Come on in."

Drake walked forward aggressively, straight to the guy who told him to get lost. The thug reached inside his jacket for his weapon but wasn't fast enough. Drake, in stride, kicked him hard in the groin, a harsh and direct hit. The thug's hands went to his crotch, and he grunted and buckled to his knees in pain, his bladder and colon likely twisting from the shock, the discomfort rising fast from his groin up into his stomach. He was teed up and waiting, unprotected, and Drake followed up with a left hook to the guy's jaw. Lights out. His eyes went blank, and he went down fast and hard like a cinder block. He sprawled out on the floor—flat, silent, and unmoving.

His buddy couldn't believe what had just happened, and he reacted fast. "What the—" He pulled out an automatic pistol, but before he could sight it on his target, Drake sidestepped, raised his right leg, and planted his foot in the middle of the guy's chest. His arm flew up and the gun fired, sending a bullet into the ceiling. The kick sent him stumbling backward three feet, and he crashed into the television.

Drake was on him fast. He punched the thug in the nose and grabbed his gun. Drake twisted the gun away from him, quick and with force, and everyone in the room—maybe even his sprawled-out buddy—could hear the sickening sound of breaking bone.

The thug screamed in pain.

Drake removed the gun from the dangling hand.

The thug went down on his knees, cradled his injured hand, and shouted at Drake, "You, you broke my fuckin' wrist." Blood dripped from his nose.

Drake stuck the gun into his waistband. Another acquisition. He stared at the guy.

The first thug was still on the ground but was coming to, shaking his head, and he tried again to reach inside his jacket.

Scotty approached him and said, "Don't be an idiot."

He stopped for just a second and looked up.

Scotty kicked him in the head with his boot, just underneath the chin, the blunt force severe and teeth-shattering, snapping the guy's head back on its post. He went back down, flat on his back, out of commission. Scotty reached down and took his gun.

Drake could see that Scotty had the situation under control. He walked over and looked down at Billy, who was balled up on the floor with his arms covering his head. "Billy, are you okay?"

Billy's arms came down, and he looked up. "Who are— Wait, I know you." He moaned and rose to a sitting position. His face was bloodied and beginning to swell, his eyes puffy. He was holding his ribs with both arms.

Drake heard rustling behind him and turned around. The thug with the broken wrist was sitting on the floor, holding his limp hand, squirming and trying to get comfortable.

"Are you crying?" Drake asked.

"Fuck you. You ain't so tough."

Drake shrugged. "What else are you packing?"

"Nothin.'"

Drake took the gun from his waistband. He stepped forward, bent down, and popped the thug on the forehead with the butt of his own gun. Then, he pointed the gun at a spot between the thug's eyes. "Ever been shot by your own gun?"

"Hey, hey. Take it easy." He gently set his broken wrist and hand down on his leg then used his other hand to reach for his left ankle.

"Easy," Drake said.

He raised the pant leg and pulled a small, .25-caliber automatic pistol from a black nylon holster that was strapped to his leg just above the top of his boot. He threw it at Drake's feet.

While keeping the gun aimed, Drake bent down, picked up the gun, and stuck it in his pocket. He watched as Scotty patted down the other guy. "I think you two are in the wrong house. Who sent you?"

The thug over by Scotty was sitting up again and spitting out pieces of teeth. "Fuck you," he said.

Drake looked at him. "Is that right?"

"You might as well go ahead and shoot me."

"I can do that for you." Drake walked over, leaned down, and put the barrel of the gun on the guy's forehead. He pushed forward with the gun.

The thug, without expression, pushed back and looked up at Drake, trying to be tough.

"Today is your lucky day," Drake said and pulled the gun away, admiring the dirty circular impression left on the guy's forehead. He stepped backward to a point equidistant from each of the thugs and toward the entryway. "Get up, both of you."

Scotty moved over toward the entryway, back and behind Drake, with a pistol in hand to cover him.

Drake turned to the one with the broken wrist and waved him over toward his buddy. "Get over there."

The thugs stood side-by-side, beaten and pathetic. It was a pitiful sight.

Drake said, "Tell your boss that I let you live. He will

not be so fortunate." Drake backed up and waved the gun toward the door. "Get out of here."

The thugs crossed the living room and ambled past Scotty and out the front door.

Drake, Scotty, and Billy remained still while they waited, and listened. They heard the sounds of car doors opening and closing, an engine starting, and a car pulling away.

Drake went over to Billy and helped him up. He was still holding his ribs and breathing through gritted teeth. Drake walked with him to a small dining area and helped him into a chair.

"Thanks," Billy said. "You're that investigator."

Drake sat down next to him. "I am."

Scotty walked over to the sofa and sat by himself.

"Do you know those guys?" Drake asked.

"Never saw them before."

"What did they want?"

"They said they heard I'd been talking about Sarah. Said I should keep my mouth shut, if I knew what was good for me. Then they started beatin' me and wouldn't let up." Billy licked his lips and wiped his mouth with the back of his hand. He saw the smeared blood on his hand and looked up at Drake, worried.

"You'll be all right. What else can you tell me?"

"Why should I talk to you?"

Drake tilted his head over to the scene of the beating. "I could call your friends back."

He considered Drake's words. The decision was an easy one. "Naw, that's all right."

"So, what else, Billy?"

Billy hugged himself, winced, and thought for a moment. His mouth twitched, and he mouthed a few silent words as he assessed the possibilities. "I think I have something they want."

"What's that?"

He looked around, like there might be someone else listening.

"It's just us. What is it? What do you have?"

Billy looked at Drake, like he wanted to say something but for some reason could not. Something was holding him back.

"It's okay. You can trust me. What is it?"

"A journal."

"What kind of journal?"

"*Sarah's* journal."

"Can I see it?"

Billy looked down and away, and it was obvious he was not sure that he wanted to fully share his secret.

"You can trust me," Drake said again.

"You'll protect me?"

Drake turned to Scotty, who nodded.

"Sure."

Billy struggled to get up and walked over to a table in the corner: the top a thin piece of oak, four spindly legs hanging down from each corner, a single drawer. He reached underneath the drawer with both hands, yanked down on a piece of tape, and pulled out a small leather journal. He held it with care, like a newly unearthed treasure, and walked back over to the table and sat down. "Like I told you. We were friends."

"How did *you* get it?"

"The day before she was—" Billy stopped. "Sorry. Let me start over. She called me, told me to meet her at the park, a few blocks down the street from her house. I rode my bike over, and she gave it to me and told me to protect it . . . forever."

Drake looked at the journal, at Billy. "Why did she give it to you?"

"Because I was her friend?" He looked to Drake for an answer.

Drake stared at him.

Billy thought about the question again, struggled for another answer. "Aw, I don't know why. I'm just a dummy."

"You're not. Maybe you were all she had, the only one who she could really trust."

"Maybe," he said, sitting up straighter. "And I kept my promise, been protectin' it ever since."

"I know."

Billy appeared embarrassed, his face flushed. "She told me not to read it, but after she disappeared, I did. I didn't think she'd mind . . . bein' dead and all. Learned a lot about her, but then, toward the end . . . It's bad . . . real bad."

"Tell me."

"After her fiancé, Matt—"

"Engel?" Drake asked.

"Yeah. After he left, Sarah was real sad. We would meet and talk, all the time. Well, she would talk. I was a good listener. Seemed to make her feel better. But then . . ."

"What?"

"Her brother, Jack, he didn't like us talkin'. He told me to stay away, or he'd beat me up. After that, after a couple days, I tried to talk to her, and she was different, acted like I wasn't there, walkin' around like she was a zombie or somethin'. And then, a couple months later, she disappeared. And I know why."

"Why?"

Billy slid the journal across the table.

Drake picked up the journal, leafed through it, and read some of the pages, but toward the middle, the book opened up and stayed open, at a place where the binding and spine had been loosened from frequent reading. He read the entry on the left side page.

Billy said, "Her brother, the alderman, did somethin' to her he shouldn't've. Couldn't believe it when I read it, but Sarah wouldn't lie. Forced himself on her, twice. Then she found out she was pregnant, *with a baby*." He shook his head and started to cry. "Who would do somethin' like that? And then . . ." He choked up and tried to hold his emotions in check, but then he started to weep.

Drake waited while Billy gained control of himself. "It's okay. Tell me."

Billy let out a couple of loud wails. He realized he was making a fuss and took a few deep breaths to calm himself.

"Listen, I can only help you if you let me."

Billy settled down and looked at Drake. "Like I said, she disappeared. Didn't call. We didn't talk. I'd go over to the house, and her brother always answered the door. Told me Sarah didn't want to see me no more. Told me never to come back." Billy wiped his nose with the length of his arm and looked at the wet streak, indifferent.

"What then?"

"I didn't believe him. I'd watch the house from a distance. The senator would leave in the morning and come back at night, but that's it. Nothin' else."

"What do you mean?"

"Nobody else ever left the house—five days straight. Then, on the fifth night, I saw the black van." Billy stopped, wiped his nose again, sniffed, and thought about what to say next.

"What black van?"

"It pulled up the driveway and around back. I couldn't see. Five minutes later, it came back out and took off down the street. Somethin' wasn't right. Just knew it." Billy became nervous, appeared scared, and his body started to tremble.

"What is it?"

Billy stared at Drake. It appeared he wasn't sure that he wanted to continue. "You got a cigarette? I could really use a cigarette."

Drake took out his pack, gave him one, and lit it. Billy took a couple of quick drags and calmed.

"What did you do?" Drake asked.

"I got on my bike and followed the van. Must've been a mile. Rode as fast as I could, all the way, to the . . . to the conservatory."

"The Lincoln Park Conservatory?"

"Yeah. It was far, but I had to. I watched it pull around the back. I ditched my bike in this tunnel at the edge of the park. Then, I crossed the park at the other end and hopped the fence into the zoo. I hid in the bushes and watched the building for most of the night."

"What did you see?"

"Not much. There were some lights on inside the building,

but that was it. I watched as long as I could, but I fell asleep under a bench." He stopped talking and smoked, slow and deliberate, like he had nothing more to say.

"That's it?"

Billy continued to smoke, ignoring Drake.

"What else?" When Billy didn't respond, Drake shouted, "Billy!"

"Yeah, yeah, okay." He took another quick drag. "I woke up in the morning. I heard somethin'. I was still lyin' on the ground, and I was so cold. *So cold.*" He hugged himself and rubbed his arms to generate warmth. "And then I saw it." His eyes filled with tears.

"What?"

"The hand. *Her* hand. Sarah's hand. Just lyin' there in the grass, like it was on display or somethin'."

"How did you know it was Sarah's?"

"The ring," Billy said. "The opal ring, from Matt. Looked like it was glowin' from the sun."

Drake said nothing and waited.

"I couldn't stop lookin' at it. I laid on the ground there for hours, just lookin'—starin' at it. Didn't make no sense. Who would do somethin' like that?" Billy cried, whimpering at first but then sobbing uncontrollably.

"I don't know," Drake said as he leaned over and put his arm around Billy. He waited until Billy calmed down. "Is there anything else?"

He sniffed and wiped his nose. "When the cops came, I took off. I hid out in a dumpster until the zoo opened, then I went home."

"Did you tell anyone?"

"Not a soul."

"Why not?"

"Couple hours after I got home, Jack came to visit me."

"The alderman?"

"Yeah," Billy said. "Told me if I ever wanted to see Sarah again, I had to keep my mouth shut."

"About what?"

"I think he was worried I knew about what he did, that Sarah told me."

"What did he do, Billy?"

"The rape."

"You know what that is?"

"I ain't stupid," Billy said as he frowned and sniffed. "He was worried and shoulda been. That son of a bitch."

"So you kept quiet?"

"A couple days later, it was killin' me, so I told my dad."

"What happened?"

"Said he'd look into it. Told me not to worry . . . and to not say a word to anyone. And so I didn't, because he woulda whipped me good. I hid the journal and never told a soul."

Drake held up the journal. "Billy, I need to take this."

"Yeah, I know. Take good care of it."

Drake pointed back over his shoulder. "My friend, Scotty, is going to stay here with you for a while, if that's all right."

Billy wiped the tears from his eyes. He looked at Scotty. "Okay."

"You're in good hands," Drake said. "He'll make sure that nothing happens to you."

"Okay."

Drake stood, put the journal into his jacket pocket, and

walked over to Scotty, who stood up. "I have a couple of visits to make."

Scotty said, "It looks like you're back in—just like the old days."

"It looks that way."

"You'll be all right on your own?"

"I'm not alone. I have you."

"Be careful."

"Yeah, careful." Drake turned, left the room, and walked out of the house.

23

After he left Billy's house, Drake drove north and east back to the South Loop area, toward the office of the second ward alderman, Jack Mitchell. Drake took full advantage of the performance capabilities of the Cougar while skirting the eyes of local authorities.

At a stoplight, Drake pulled out his phone and dialed Karen's number. He had a few minutes until he would arrive at the alderman's office, and he needed to find out if she had heard anything about their daughter. The light turned green, and he hit the accelerator. After three rings she answered the call.

"Hi," Drake said.

"Sebastian, have you found her?"

Drake had his answer in her response, but not the one he was hoping for. "I'm out looking right now. Don't worry, we'll get her back."

"I'm so scared. I can only imagine how Samantha feels. I feel so helpless. I don't know what to do."

"Just stay home, in case she shows up or if the authorities need to reach you."

"They're all over," she said.

"Who?"

"The authorities: the local police, the FBI, and some group I've never heard of. I overheard one of them talking. I think he said M-D-A. He said he 'owed you.' What does *that* mean?"

Drake said nothing but stared ahead and continued driving. He couldn't tell her that the MDA, the Munitions Development Agency, was a sub-branch of the CIA that focused on the development of new weapons and ammunition. He couldn't tell her it was also the organization that first hired him after he graduated from college. He couldn't tell her that he had worked for the Agency on a highly classified project, had been given Top Secret security clearance, and had completed the service for his country in an honorable manner, albeit with an abrupt and premature ending. She never knew. No one ever knew.

There were two people who knew Drake better than anyone: his friend, Scotty, and his ex-wife, Karen. They both knew him well, but each of them had different and incomplete knowledge. The only person who knew the complete story was Drake himself.

"Sebastian?"

"I called in a favor," Drake said. "It's a long story, but let them help. Listen, I have to run. I'll talk to you later, and don't worry, we'll find her." He hung up and put the phone into his pocket. He floored the accelerator and took off.

* * *

Drake arrived at Alderman Mitchell's office about ten minutes later and parked in front of the building, which was located at the far south border of the second ward. It was a rehabbed commercial building that accommodated small business enterprises and private practices. Drake knew the alderman had picked the location because it was within the ward boundaries and close to his new condo building on the east side of Michigan Avenue. He entered the lobby of the building and took the stairs two at a time up to the second floor.

The alderman's office was down at the far end of the hall and was distinguishable from the dozen or so offices Drake passed along the way. Based on the office facade, the entryway, and what was visible, it looked like the alderman was putting his campaign donations to good use, to put a professional-looking face on the operation: a floor-to-ceiling glass door that bisected a wood-paneled wall, high-end leather furniture, and a sleek and modern wood reception desk. Drake walked through the glass door. Behind the desk were several cubicles and a long hallway. In the back corner was an enclosed, glass-walled office. Drake saw Alderman Mitchell through the glass, standing and holding court in front of several people.

Drake walked up to the reception desk.

The young man sitting behind the desk looked up. "Good afternoon, may I help you?"

"I'm here to see Alderman Mitchell."

"Do you have an appointment?"

"Yes, I'm Mr. Drake. He's expecting me."

He consulted his computer screen. "I'm sorry, I don't see you on the calendar for today."

"I just confirmed it with him this afternoon."

The young man assessed Drake and thought for a moment. He was not convinced that Drake was telling the truth, and he pointed to the couch against the wall. "If you'll have a seat, I'll check to see if he's in."

Drake stood firm and said nothing. He watched as the man picked up the phone and dialed a number. He spun around on his chair, his back now to Drake, in an attempt to keep his conversation more private. Drake walked past him and down the aisle toward the back office.

The young man likely saw a flash in his peripheral vision. "Wait. No. Excuse me. You can't go back there."

Drake ignored him and continued walking.

"Sir!" He bolted from his chair and followed Drake.

Drake approached the alderman's office and opened the door in stride. The crowd inside looked at him curiously. He ignored them.

Alderman Mitchell met Drake's gaze. He smiled then returned his attention to the people in his office. "Can you all excuse me for a minute?"

The people reacted, most with surprise, some appearing inconvenienced, but they all stood up and filed out past Drake.

Calmly, the alderman said, "Thank you. We'll continue our meeting later."

The receptionist stepped into the doorway next to Drake, was noticeably flustered. "Alderman Mitchell, I'm so sorry. He just barged in."

"It's all right. I'll meet with Mr. Drake."

Concerned but accepting his defeat, the receptionist turned around and walked away, likely wondering if his job had just become less secure.

The alderman watched him leave, and when he was a sufficient distance away, he said, "Mr. Drake, please come in."

Alderman Mitchell walked behind his desk and sat down. Drake sat down across from him.

"Mr. Drake, I've only met you twice now, and I'm quite sure I don't like you."

Drake glared at him.

"I'm also sure you're here for a reason, so let's get to it and make it quick."

"I should kill you right now."

The alderman reached for the phone.

Drake opened his jacket just enough so the alderman could see the pistol in his holster. "I wouldn't do that."

Alderman Mitchell froze.

"I spoke with Billy Taylor today," Drake said. "I'm quite sure *he* doesn't like *you*."

The alderman sat back and rested his hands in his lap.

"I know all about you and Sarah. I can't imagine that the publicity of your inappropriate relationship with her would be helpful to your political career."

"You don't know shit," the alderman said.

Drake reached into his pocket and pulled out the journal. He showed it to Alderman Mitchell. "Look familiar?"

"No." The alderman stared at it. "It looks like a journal. So what?"

"It's Sarah's journal."

"I don't think so."

"It's quite revealing," Drake said. "You should be ashamed of yourself."

"I don't know what you're talking about."

"You took advantage of your own sister. Flesh and blood. Incest. You're a sick man."

Alderman Mitchell's face flushed. "I don't need to listen to this. Get out."

"I think you do. You had your way with her, she became pregnant, and then you had a big problem on your hands. My guess is that you killed her and made the issue go away. But not really."

Alderman Mitchell became enraged, ejected himself from his chair.

Drake pulled his gun in a flash, held it close at chest level, and pointed it at the alderman's heart. "Sit down."

The alderman tensed, ground his teeth, and sat back down.

Drake could see the muscles in the alderman's jaw, bulging and quivering, and a film of sweat glistening on his forehead. "Not only do I think you were involved in her murder, I think you and your family have not been pleased with my recent involvement in the case. I've stirred up some old feelings. I've opened the can of worms again. You need me to go away, and what do you know, this morning, my daughter disappeared."

"I don't know what you're talking about," the alderman said again, unsettled.

"Where is she?"

"Really, I—I don't know."

Drake raised the gun, leveled it eye-to-eye, and aimed it at the alderman's forehead. "I'm going to make you a deal, Alderman, and it's only good for one day—today." Drake paused.

"I'm listening."

"I want my daughter back, without a scratch, now. If you do that, you get the journal, and I go away. Case closed."

"How can I trust you?"

"I'm going to walk out of here and not kill you."

The alderman considered his predicament, licked his lips, and cleared his throat. "And the journal?"

Drake put the journal back into his pocket. He pulled out a business card and set it on the desk.

The alderman picked up the card and studied it, considering what to do or say next. "Let me look into your allegations. I'll call you."

"I want her home, now. You have an hour." He watched the expression on Alderman Mitchell's face change.

The alderman looked scared, and his eyes had glazed over, his mind off in some other place.

"Alderman! Do you understand me?"

"Yeah," the alderman said. He was quiet, thoughtful, and gazing past Drake. "An hour."

Drake put the gun back into its holster, stood up, and left the alderman's office.

* * *

Drake exited the building wondering if he had made any progress at all. He lit a cigarette, looked up and down the street, and contemplated his next move. Before he could decide, his phone rang, and he pulled it from his inside coat pocket fast, as though drawing his gun. "Hello, this is Drake."

"Mr. Drake, this is Chief Peters."

Drake listened, said nothing.

"I am aware of your daughter's disappearance," the chief said.

"How?"

"That's not important. I want to help. I'm the one who contacted the authorities, to get them involved to help search for your daughter."

"Okay. Thanks."

"Do you think your daughter's disappearance has something to do with your investigation?"

Again, Drake said nothing.

"I do," Chief Peters said. "Can you come by the station? I'd like to talk to you about the approach we're taking to find Samantha."

"I don't have time."

"Please. It will just take a few minutes."

Drake drew on his cigarette and considered the request. He felt his meeting with the alderman had gone well and, with the journal, had provided the appropriate amount of leverage. He looked at his watch. He'd given the alderman an hour to deliver his daughter, a reasonable amount of time to satisfy his request, and he wondered if he could spare a few minutes—just to cover his bases and possibly have a backup plan in case the alderman had a change of heart. He looked up and down the street again but at nothing in particular. "I'm over in the South Loop. I'll be there in twenty minutes."

"I'll see you then," Chief Peters said.

Drake ended the call. He hurried to his car, slid in, and sped away.

* * *

As soon as Drake had left the building, Alderman Mitchell closed the door to his office then walked over and yanked on a string, which closed the blinds tight and shielded him from the office staff. He walked back over to his desk and sat down; his moves were measured and calculated, like a robot. The room was silent. He pulled a sheet of paper from his desk drawer, took the pen from his desktop set, and wrote a few lines on the page as though practicing penmanship. He put the pen back and folded the sheet of paper into a neat square that fit in his shirt pocket. He opened his lower desk drawer and pulled out a gun. It was a huge revolver: a Ruger Redhawk, silver with wood grips, and a five-and-a-half inch barrel. It overshadowed his small hands. He felt the weight of the gun in both hands and stared at it as though it was alien to him. He raised the gun but stopped, overcome with emotion, and although he tried to hold it back, he broke down and began to sob. After a minute, he collected himself then stared at the gun again, caressing the wood grips and feeling the smooth cold steel. He raised the gun, wobbling in his shaking hands, and put the barrel end into his mouth.

The alderman's eyes were wide open, glazed, and blinking erratically.

A single tear dripped from his left eye.

* * *

Traffic was light, and Drake made it to the police station in less than fifteen minutes. He parked in front of the station, illegally, and hurried through the front door. The watch commander was expecting him, and he had a patrolman escort Drake to Chief Peters' office.

Drake stood in the doorway of the office before going in. "Chief?"

"Mr. Drake, please come in."

Sitting across from Chief Peters was Detective Hartman, who glared at Drake, cold and apparently disgruntled about something. Drake sat down next to him.

"You remember Detective Hartman?"

"I do."

"Thanks for coming so quickly. Once I heard about your daughter, I checked with the municipal police department and told them they have our full support. I have two cars deployed to help them with their search. I also called in the FBI."

"Why is that?"

"I have a dead detective and a kidnapped girl, all in the span of a couple of days, and the events are possibly related to a cold murder case affecting one of the most powerful and prominent families in the state."

The phone on the chief's desk rang. He picked up the handset. "Peters." He listened and expressed concern, his brows furrowed and eyes squinted. "Okay. You've talked to the staff?" He listened again. "Really. Okay. Keep everyone away from the scene until Hartman gets there. What about the media?" He listened then huffed. "Shit."

The chief set the handset down on the console then leaned forward on his desk, hands folded, his knuckles white. "Alderman Jack Mitchell is dead. An apparent suicide." The chief stared at Drake.

Drake sat still and stone-faced.

"Holy shit," Hartman said. "I don't believe it."

Chief Peters said, "It seems he wrote a suicide note and stuck it in his shirt pocket. Then he took a .44-Magnum revolver and stuck it in his mouth. I guess he wanted to be certain there was nothing left of him. His brains are on display on the wall of his office."

The chief continued to stare at Drake. "And you were just there to visit him."

"I'm sure they told you he was very much alive when I left."

"Why did you go to see him?"

"To make a contribution to his campaign fund."

"Bullshit," Chief Peters said. "What kind of gun are you carrying?"

Drake opened his jacket. There was nothing there but his shirt. "I'm a writer. All I need is a pen."

"You're a real smart ass," Hartman said. "I ought to—"

Chief Peters raised a hand and interrupted him. "Mike, get over to Alderman Mitchell's office right away. I want you to take the lead on this."

Hartman grunted, but he obeyed his orders and stood up. "And him?" he asked, hooking a thumb toward Drake.

"I'll take care of him," Chief Peters said.

Hartman slid by Drake and walked out.

Chief Peters watched Hartman leave then turned back to Drake. "I ought to lock you up right now."

"You know I didn't do it," Drake said.

"Things were quiet around here, and then *you* came along."

"Quiet? You had fifty murders last week."

The chief could not argue. "What *aren't* you telling me, Mr. Drake?"

"Listen, I just want my daughter back. I'm off the Mitchell case. It's your problem now."

The chief seemed pleased with this latest development. "All right. Get out of here while you still can."

"Keep in touch," Drake said, rising from his chair.

The chief measured Drake, looked him over, then yelled, "Jackson, get in here." The chief reclined back in his chair, a worried expression on his face, and pondered his newest dilemma. "Go on, get out of here."

Drake walked out of the office.

24

Drake sat in the idling Cougar with his hands on the wheel, staring out through the windshield and thinking about the alderman's sudden and unexpected demise. A feeling of anxiety swelled in his chest because, with the alderman out of the picture, the fate of his daughter was slipping out of his grasp, and he had left Chief Peters' office without a backup plan.

Before getting back in the car, he had retrieved his holster from the trunk and put it back on. *Almost there.* He reached into the glove compartment and pulled out his gun. He ejected and checked the magazine again: eight bullets, *his* bullets. He thumbed one of the bullets out of the magazine and into his other hand. He looked down at the bullet as thoughts of his earlier days with the Agency came roaring back. *It's time to finish the job.* He loaded the bullet into the magazine, put the magazine back into the gun, and returned the gun to its holster.

Drake shifted the car into gear and took off down the street.

As dusk blanketed the city and the street lights came on, Drake pulled up in front of Jerry Fitzsimmons' house. He was out of the car and up the front stairs in a few long strides.

He would have preferred to just kick the door in, but not wanting to attract attention, he rang the doorbell instead.

An exceptionally tall and wide gentleman, dressed in a black suit and mock turtleneck, opened the door. His dark hair was cut close to the scalp, and his nose was spread, broad and flat, on his face. It seemed his neck was as thick as his thigh. Drake stood before him, calm and twirling his key ring around his finger.

"Can I help you?" the man asked in a deep, baritone voice. He appeared to be inconvenienced.

"I'm here to see Mr. Fitzsimmons."

"No, you're not."

Drake glared at the man, unflinching, and waited. He heard footsteps.

"Let him in," Fitzsimmons said from down the hall.

The man in the black suit stepped aside and held the door open.

Drake crossed the threshold, peered down the hall, and saw Fitzsimmons standing there, an odd smirk on his face. Drake walked in, and, just as he passed the big black suit, the man grabbed him by one arm and threw him against the wall. It was a quick and violent blow, but it was uncontrolled. Drake hit the wall, took the full impact in his chest and left shoulder, and bounced off. Taking advantage of the momentum, he swiftly turned and in one fluid and rapid motion, he swung his arm around and, like a piston, thrust his car key into the man's throat. With his other hand, Drake drew his gun and sighted it on Fitzsimmons down the hall.

The man in black reacted with a combined expression of

pain, surprise, and fear. A lethal neck wound from a blunt metal instrument will do that to a man. The man's hands went to his throat and he wheezed and pleaded with his wet and bulging eyes. Blood squirted out from between his fingers. The man collapsed to the floor as the wheezing from his throat changed to a sickening, gurgling sound.

Drake faced Fitzsimmons, who had a revolver in his hand.

"Bravo, Mr. Drake. A key to the throat, to the jugular to be precise. I can't say that I've ever seen that particular move executed before. Is that a standard CIA tactic?"

Drake put the keys into his jacket pocket. He clenched his jaw tight, kept his gun aimed steady on Fitzsimmons, and chose not to respond.

Fitzsimmons said, "You went to a lot of trouble to keep your past life a secret. Unfortunately, your government has let certain security protocols lapse. Do you think the CIA cares at all about your worthless life?" His thin lips pressed together tight like a cadaver.

"I know they won't care if I kill *you*."

Fitzsimmons parted his lips, showed yellow teeth. "The Munitions Development Agency: from what I've learned, what you were doing had promise—developing high-tech ammunition to increase kill rate efficiency and protect those who serve our country. You were held in high regard for your shooting skills, your expert marksmanship. Yes, you had promise. That is, until they asked you to test one of their creations as part of a covert operation. That is, until you killed the wrong person."

"I assure you, I killed the right person."

"But with collateral damage. An innocent young woman.

The political backlash was too much to bear. You took the fall, and they shut down the program."

The muscles in Drake's neck tightened. Fitzsimmons was, for the most part, accurate in his understanding, and Drake wondered how a lowlife like him might have learned about his past.

* * *

Fitzsimmons was referring to an assignment Drake accepted at an earlier time in his life, a time in his early twenties when a man is most confident and feels almost invincible. Drake was in the field, in a war-torn Middle Eastern country he had no business being in, when the lines of communication and intelligence broke down and he was forced for the second time to make a decision to save his and Scotty's lives.

On that particular assignment, Drake and Scotty were in an open market, had tailed their target to that location based on Agency intelligence. Scotty had confirmed the identity of their target, and Drake had called in for authorization to terminate, following protocol. The location wasn't perfect or preferred, but *he had a clear shot, would only need one*, he had told them. Drake was twenty yards away, his pistol raised and sighted. Scotty was in position behind a parked car, his gun drawn, covering Drake. Before Drake received the go-ahead, they were spotted and, in an instant, all hell broke loose. Their target, a thirty-year-old leader of a terrorist cell responsible for the deaths of eighty-four Americans, had pulled out an Uzi submachine gun and started shooting into the crowd. People were screaming and running in all directions. Some hit the dirt or ducked into tents. Drake had lost his shot. The terrorist emptied a magazine into the crowd and pulled another to reload. Drake, Scotty, and the terrorist stood out in the mostly cleared market like points on a triangle. There were dozens of dead and injured people on the ground and everyone else had taken cover. Drake had his clear shot again but still no clearance to execute. The terrorist loaded a new magazine, made eye contact with Drake, and winked. He must have thought that Drake would not—or could not—take the shot. He was wrong. Drake pulled the trigger and shot the terrorist in the middle of his forehead, and he dropped like a bag of sand.

The bullet in Drake's gun, not his preferred round but the one he was ordered to use, was designed to penetrate and scramble, turning the brain to mush. Unfortunately, a part of the projectile remained intact, exited the back of the terrorist's skull, and hit a civilian, a young woman who was in the wrong place at the wrong time, who had run from a tent and behind the terrorist at the last minute in an effort to flee.

The negative media attention and resulting political backlash was a handful for the Agency to manage, but the impact to Drake was more severe. He was devastated. He shut down. Depressed and guilt-ridden, Drake submitted his resignation the following week. He was determined to leave it all behind to pursue a new life, months later taking a job as a reporter with the *Chicago Tribune*.

Colonel Roger Masterson, the man who had recruited Drake and had recommended him for the MDA, had learned of Drake's situation and had arranged the job at the *Tribune*, a seemingly impossible task given the state of the newspaper industry. However, the editor of the newspaper was a Vietnam veteran, had served as a member of Masterson's platoon, and Masterson called in a favor, sold the editor on Drake's journalism education at Northwestern and his investigation and writing experience at the government that had never transpired. It was one war buddy helping another, and the editor created a position for Drake and helped to work him into the current staff of experienced, hardened, and competitive reporters.

After an extensive investigation and analysis of the facts, Drake was cleared of any fault. His government file was supposedly expunged, cleansed to make it look as though he never existed, and three weeks later, the entire program was shut down, files sealed and personnel reassigned.

Drake had always accepted the risk that, at some point in his life, details of his time with the Agency might be revealed. However, in all the years since he had walked away, he had never considered what he would do in the event it happened . . . not until now. The dam was breached, and he needed to patch it, fast, for if not, the resulting damage could be severe.

* * *

"You watch too much TV," Drake said.

"Like I said, they don't care about you," Fitzsimmons said, his gun still pointed.

Drake kept his gun on Fitzsimmons, but he looked down at the man on the ground and listened to assess his condition. The big man's gurgling had slowed to a bubbling whisper, and there were longer spaces between breaths. The pool of blood grew larger around his head like a thick crimson halo. Then all sounds from the man ceased.

Fitzsimmons said, "That wasn't very nice of you."

They were caught in a standoff, staring at each other and, if looks could kill, they would both likely be dead. They were fifteen feet apart, a comfortable—and in most cases, lethal—shooting distance, and they remained standing fixed with their guns pointed.

Fitzsimmons broke first, put his gun in the pocket of his cardigan sweater, and walked down the hall. "Why don't we go into the library, Mr. Drake."

Drake kept his gun aimed at the back of Fitzsimmons' head and followed him into the library.

Fitzsimmons walked over and sat down in his high-back chair. He crossed his legs and folded his hands in his lap, as if he was waiting for the opera to begin, appearing carefree and unconcerned.

Drake approached until he was ten feet away and stopped. He put his gun back into its holster then turned around to look at the flowers on the table.

"Again, you're interested in the flowers," Fitzsimmons said.

Drake turned back.

"Since this will be our last meeting, Mr. Drake, why don't you tell me what's on your mind."

"I appreciate you sending me back to Billy Taylor. Your poker face was weak. I knew you would send your goons over to keep him quiet."

"My men told me about your meeting." He shook his head, expressed disappointment. "It's getting so hard to find good help these days."

"It seems you didn't try too hard."

"You may be right."

"Billy showed me Sarah Mitchell's journal. All the details about how her brother raped her. The pregnancy. But you know all that. I confronted the alderman this afternoon about the journal, about the incest. He didn't take it too well. You know he's dead?"

"I heard. That's one less problem for me to deal with—one less mess to clean up. He was such a pompous and conceited little bastard."

"And while his crime was despicable," Drake said, "your crime was worse. The family couldn't be tarnished with news like that: incest, a pregnant daughter, the scandal."

"Indeed."

"And so they called you in to clean up, the mess, as you call it. Who gave the order, Senator Mitchell?"

Fitzsimmons forced a smile. "He really was a great politician, cared only about *the people*. No, he didn't have a clue."

"Then who?"

"I wasn't going to let that little problem get in the way of me getting what I deserved. That scandal would have ruined the senator, the family. It would have ruined me."

"So you killed her."

"Mr. Drake, I believe our meeting is over."

"Where's my daughter?"

"You had to go and get involved in our family business," Fitzsimmons said.

"It's not *your* family," Drake said. "You're just a hired hand. An employee. Where's my daughter?"

"Where's the journal, Mr. Drake?"

Drake drew his gun and aimed it. His demeanor mirrored the cold steel of the gun.

Fitzsimmons didn't flinch. "You won't shoot me; you're not that stupid. I'm the one who determines if your daughter lives or dies."

"The flowers you keep in your home, you can't get them at your local florist."

"What are you talking about?" Fitzsimmons asked, now growing uneasy.

"Your obsession with flowers—very manly," Drake said with a hint of sarcasm, "and quite revealing."

An expression of surprise crossed Fitzsimmons' face. His mouth twitched with contempt then he huffed in frustration. He jerked and reached into his sweater pocket for his gun.

Drake anticipated the move. With the front sight locked on target, and as he had done thousands of times before, he slowly released his breath, paused, and squeezed the trigger. The gun fired, the explosion muted. Drake felt a gentle recoil that did not interrupt his sightline, and his gun did not eject a bullet casing; within a second, the combustion process effectively broke down and disintegrated the organic structure of the casing, as designed. *No loose ends.* A faint swirl of vapor rose from the barrel.

In that same second, the projectile hit Fitzsimmons at the bridge of his nose and between the eyes. His head flew back, his face frozen in a mask of surprise and horror.

Drake stood for a moment, gun still pointed, staring at Fitzsimmons, what remained of him. Fitzsimmons' neck gave way and his head collapsed, tilted back and to the side, until it rested in the corner of the wingback. He stiffened, was motionless in his chair. Blood dripped from the bullet hole and down the bridge of his nose.

Drake holstered his gun. He approached Fitzsimmons and stared for a moment at the frozen face, the mouth agape. There was no need to check for a pulse. He leaned in close and noticed a smear of white powder on the sleeve of Fitzsimmons' sweater. Drake touched the smear, rubbed the powdery substance between his fingers, and smelled them. *Flowers.*

Drake straightened. In an instant, the smell of the flowery powder on his fingers had fired synapses, triggered a series of mental connections: individual ideas now linked together as fact, a theory proven and substantiated, dots from Engel's research and his own now connected, creating something more meaningful.

It all fell into place.

25

Drake took the ramp onto Lake Shore Drive and headed north, driving fast but controlled and determined. He turned left on La Salle then right on Stockton Drive, continuing north.

Upon arriving at the Lincoln Park Conservatory, he parked in the rear lot and entered the building through the back door. It was locked, but the doorjamb was loose and soft and gave way to his shoulder. The room smelled of moist earth, and the high humidity hit Drake in the face like a wet blanket. He ran through what looked like a gardener's work area, a dozen steel tables littered with planters, tools, and dirt. He opened a sliding door at the far end of the work area, proceeded down a short hallway, and hurried into the large, main vestibule of the conservatory. It resembled a manicured jungle. A few fixtures hanging from the ceiling of the glass roof lit the room. Small cement paths cut through the seemingly endless foliage displays in every direction.

Drake took the path to his left, leading toward the east side of the conservatory. The path led him to a smaller, semi-enclosed room displaying more plants. Inside the room, he found his daughter, Samantha, sitting on a chair with her hands tied behind the back of it. Clarisse Mitchell was standing behind the chair, appearing innocent and proper, as though she was at a staged political event, a hand on Samantha's shoulder.

"Daddy!"

"I'm impressed, Mr. Drake," Clarisse said. "It seems you are a more capable foe than I expected."

Drake heard nothing as he rushed over to his daughter. He stood before her and glared at Clarisse, his eyes telling her to *back off*. She did and promptly stepped backward and away from the chair and walked around to the other side of the room, creating some distance between them.

Drake knelt down in front of Samantha. "Hey, baby, are you okay?"

"I'm okay."

Drake saw that she was scared but putting up a strong front. She looked physically fine.

Clarisse said, "You've caused irreparable harm to my family, Mr. Drake."

Again, Drake heard nothing and paid no attention as he untied Samantha from the chair. When she was free, he stood and turned to face Clarisse. "You're going to prison," he said.

Clarisse chuckled and swept her bangs back from her forehead. "You're too funny, Mr. Drake. I was expecting Mr. Fitzsimmons, but apparently, he was not up for the challenge."

"He's at home, taking a long nap."

"I'm sure he is."

"Why did you do it?"

"Whatever are you talking about?"

"Your daughter, the murder."

"I didn't murder my daughter, Mr. Drake. That would be barbaric, wrong in every possible sense. We have people to take care of business like that."

"Fitzsimmons," Drake said.

Clarisse smiled. "I can't put one past *you*."

"But why?"

"I loved my daughter. She was my baby, a child prodigy, about to take the world by storm with her musical talents. Ready to make her family proud."

"But your son had other plans."

"Yes, unfortunately, my son was a sick boy."

"He was deranged, and he should have been locked up," Drake said.

She thought for a moment, gazing at Drake, but he could tell she was not seeing him. "Yes, I suppose you are correct, and now he has accepted responsibility for his actions by taking his own life."

"You had your daughter murdered."

"Mr. Drake, you have to understand. I came from simple beginnings. I grew up in a small town. We had nothing. When I was finally able to get out of that God-forsaken place, I knew that I was never going to let anyone or anything stop me from getting what I deserved. When I had the opportunity to meet the senator, I knew he would be mine. And all I had to do then was protect the family. Can you imagine what would have happened if word got out, about the incest, the pregnancy? We would have been ruined. *I* would have been ruined."

"You're pathetic."

"It was a difficult decision, but I did it to protect the family."

"You did it to protect yourself."

Clarisse sneered, devilishly, as if accepting the words as truth.

"And now, as I said, Mrs. Mitchell, you're going to prison."

Detective Hartman stepped out from behind the wall partition. "I don't think she'll be going anywhere." He had a revolver in his hand, leveled and pointed at Drake.

Drake was caught off guard. Clarisse was not.

"Hartman," Drake said.

"Drake, Drake. I never thought it would come to this, but it seems it has come to this." Hartman scowled at Drake with narrowed dark eyes, his right eyebrow twitching.

"But why?" Drake asked, though he knew the answer.

"I have to look out for myself."

"By being a crony for the Mitchell family?"

Nonchalantly, Hartman said, "The money's good. But you wouldn't understand, and even if you did, I could give a shit."

"And Angie?"

"Poor Angie. Her death was unfortunate, but necessary," Hartman said. "She was a nice kid, but a little too aggressive, wouldn't you say?" He raised an eyebrow and grinned like a deviant.

"I'll see if we can get you and Mrs. Mitchell adjoining cells," Drake said.

Hartman laughed. "You can see that I have a gun pointed at your chest, can't you?"

With one arm, Drake moved his daughter behind him, shielding her. "Baby, I want you to close your eyes and cover your ears, okay."

"Okay, Daddy," Samantha said.

"Eyes closed, ears covered tight?"

She didn't respond.

Drake whispered, "Good girl."

Hartman asked, "What I don't get is, why get back into the business?"

Drake stared at Hartman.

"I don't see you for years, and then you show up on my doorstep. You think I'm not going to do my homework, not going to check you out? I know all about your government work, *Sebastian*. Your background, it's quite impressive. I never would have guessed. And I should have taken care of you the first day I saw you again. I knew you were going to be trouble, a royal pain in the ass." Hartman walked toward Drake, slow and cautious, his gun still pointed on target. "Don't worry, I'll make it quick."

Just as the last word, *quick*, came out of Hartman's mouth, the watering system switched on automatically with a *clunk*, air hissing and water squirting through tiny holes from sprinkler heads on the ceiling and in the plant beds. Hartman flinched and looked up toward the ceiling, the sound and the spraying mist distracting him for just a second.

In that same moment, Drake pulled his Walther, aimed, and fired a single shot. Though muted, the sound echoed in the small room.

The bullet hit Hartman in the middle of his chest, a direct hit to his heart. His arms flew wide then he froze. He looked down at his chest, bewildered, as he saw the growing burgundy spot on his shirt. A thought came to him, and he appeared enlightened. His head rose, and he flashed the grin and stare of the devil.

Drake was surprised that Hartman was still standing but figured he would not be for long. He knew Hartman likely felt a jolt of searing pain in his chest, for just a second, as a vision of white lightening flashed in his eyes while his heart's electrical system experienced a life-ending short circuit and his last heartbeat became a lost memory.

Drake said, "I don't need the second shot," as he saw Hartman's gun hand rise and swing around toward him. "But . . ."

Drake, his gun arm still fixed and pointed at Hartman but with the gun now locked on a new target, released his breath, paused, and squeezed off a second shot. Again, the sound of the gunshot reverberated throughout the room, and a light haze of smoke-like vapor hung in the air.

After Drake had squeezed the trigger, all at once his hand, wrist, and arm absorbed the slight recoil and his eyes sighted a small, black hole that appeared in the middle of Hartman's forehead. Drake watched the hole as it leaked blood that trickled down and spilled past the tip of Hartman's nose and over his lips.

"But you're worth it."

Hartman's evil gaze was replaced with the thoughtless expression of a cold zombie as he fell backward like a plank of wood into the dense, wet foliage. The jungle of a display had swallowed him up. Only his feet remained visible.

Clarisse and Drake appeared unaffected by Hartman's demise and stood still in the room, being sprayed, assessing the situation, and calculating their next moves. Samantha was crouched behind her father, her eyes still squeezed tight and her hands pressed against her ears. Drake reached behind and put a hand on her shoulder, to let her know that everything was all right, and he could feel her shaking. Drake and Clarisse waited for the sound repercussions of the last shot to subside until the room was filled only with the sound of spraying water.

"Thank you, Mr. Drake, for relieving me of the task of having to deal with him. You seem to be tying up all of my loose ends for me." She appeared composed and confident. "What do you have planned next?"

Drake swung his arm and pointed his gun at Clarisse.

"You won't kill me," she said. "I'm the reason your daughter is alive."

"She was bait, to get to me. Once I was dead, you would have killed her. Just like Sarah."

"Fitzsimmons, he wanted to bury your daughter here from the start, as a companion for Sarah."

"I have just one question," Drake said.

"And what is that?"

"Why the hand? Why, for God's sake, would you cut off your daughter's hand?"

She sighed. An expression of serenity seemed to come over her as she said, "Sometimes, in life, a problem tends to get worse before it gets better. Unbeknownst to me, Mr. Fitzsimmons had thought it was a good idea. Then my son agreed with him. *Idiots*. Fitzsimmons obtained the tools from a doctor friend of his, and that's all Jack Junior needed. Actually, I think my son was always jealous of his sister. Maybe it was his way of making a statement." She shook her head, suddenly disgusted. "Like I said, he was a sick boy."

"And the senator?"

"What about him?"

"He was in on all of this?"

"My dear husband," Clarisse said. "He was a wonderful man, a terrific leader." She paused. "And he didn't have a clue."

No one spoke. The watering system switched off, and the lingering silence was replaced by the escalating sound of an approaching siren. Flashing lights entered the room through the glass walls, bouncing around like a strobe light.

"Mr. Drake, it's been a pleasure," Clarisse said as she reached into her jacket pocket. She pulled out a small inhaler and looked at it. She licked her lips, seductively, and glanced up at Drake. She put the inhaler into her mouth, squeezed it, and inhaled its contents.

Drake watched her, his arm still raised, his gun still pointed. She winked at him.

He heard footsteps, and Chief Peters entered the room. "Freeze! Drop the gun!"

Drake looked over and saw that Chief Peters' gun was pointed at him. Drake bent down and set his gun on the ground. He straightened, and kicked the gun away.

"Mrs. Mitchell, are you all right?" Chief Peters asked.

Disoriented, Clarisse said, "I *have* felt better." Her eyes glazed over, and a blank expression crossed her face. Her knees buckled, and she collapsed to the floor.

Chief Peters ran to her while keeping his gun pointed at

Drake. He knelt down and reached for her neck. He moved his fingers around every couple of seconds, searching for a pulse, and he lowered his ear to her mouth and listened for a long time. "She's dead."

"Seems it was more excitement than she could handle," Drake said.

Chief Peters stood up, his gun still pointed at Drake. He looked over and saw the feet sticking out from the bed of plants. He looked at Drake.

"Hartman," Drake said.

The chief didn't react, as though he already knew.

"He's a bad cop."

"I know. I came here to arrest him."

They assessed each other.

The chief asked, "Do you happen to know the whereabouts of Mr. Fitzsimmons?"

"I heard he's at home, resting."

Chief Peters lowered his gun and put it back into his belt holster.

Drake turned around, stooped, and held his daughter's head, looking at her closed eyes. He pulled her hands away from her ears. "It's okay, baby."

Samantha opened her eyes, saw her father's face, and beamed.

They hugged and held each other for a long time.

Drake looked over at Chief Peters, who stepped forward and picked up his gun.

"You won't mind if I hold on to this?"

Drake shook his head. "It's all yours."

Chief Peters said, "I've had my eye on Hartman for a while.

But after Detective Parker's murder, I put twenty-four hour surveillance on him. He's not too bright, practically drew me a map to this place. I couldn't quite believe it though. That's why I had to come myself."

Drake nodded.

"You, we, have some explaining to do."

"I figure."

"I'll need you to come down to the station. We have some matters to untangle."

"Of course."

"And I'll need you to put these on." Chief Peters tossed a pair of handcuffs to Drake.

He caught them and put them on. He looked down at Samantha. "Everything will be fine."

"I know, Daddy."

Chief Peters said, "And we'll have a squad car take your daughter home."

Drake bent down, held Samantha's face in his cuffed hands, and looked into her eyes, concerned.

"It's all right, Daddy. I'm a big girl," she said.

Drake smiled. "You certainly are."

The chief looked once more at the dead bodies, the scene. It appeared nothing surprised him any more. He took out his phone and dialed a number. "Hello, this is Chief Peters. Send a patrol car and the medical examiner over to the Lincoln Park Conservatory."

"Unbelievable," he said to Drake.

"I'll say."

"Well, let's get out of here," the chief said as he walked toward the exit.

Samantha hooked a hand around Drake's arm, and he led her out of the room.

26

A Chicago Metro Police squad car pulled up in front of Karen Drake's house. The police officer in the passenger seat exited the car and opened the rear door. He helped Samantha out of the car and held her by the hand.

The door of the house opened, and Karen ran out and down the walkway. Samantha let go of the police officer and ran to her. They held each other and cried.

Ted, Karen's boyfriend, walked out the front door with Samantha's sister, Kelly, in tow. Together, they hurried down the walkway and joined in the hug. It was later in the evening, the street was quiet, and no one noticed.

* * *

Drake sat in the interrogation room at the police station, a cold room he had become familiar with, although not intentionally. He looked at his watch and could not believe the time. He tapped the face of the watch a few times and raised it to his ear to listen. It was an antique watch from the nineteen forties with an art deco styled case that Karen had given him as a gift many years ago. It still ticked and seemed to show the correct time. Drake thought of Karen and smiled.

He pulled out his pack of cigarettes, reached to take one but decided not to, and put the pack back into his pocket. He still had his cigarettes, still had everything. They had not searched, charged, or fingerprinted him. When they arrived at the station, Chief Peters had taken him to the interrogation room, removed the cuffs, and told him to wait. That was two hours ago.

There was a knock on the door, then the door opened. Ray Parsons walked in.

Drake wasn't surprised and welcomed the familiar face.

"The chief called me," Parsons said. "He has a lot of dead bodies to account for, needs someone to be responsible. He may have to charge you with the murders of Clarisse Mitchell, Jerry Fitzsimmons, and Detective Hartman."

Drake said nothing.

"You're in a world of shit, my friend." He looked at Drake, and it appeared as though maybe Parsons felt sorry for him, or understood, or maybe just cared—because they had once been friends. "I called a good friend of mine. He'll be here shortly to represent you."

"That won't be necessary."

"Drake, this is serious. We're just waiting on the reports from the medical examiner and the ballistics lab. You've been placed at the scenes, that evidence indisputable. You went to Fitzsimmons' house, you left, and we found him dead. From there, you went to the conservatory, Hartman and Clarisse Mitchell were there, and they both ended up dead. It's quite a record of accomplishment. You're going to be charged, and you need a lawyer."

Chief Peters walked into the room. His face reflected an

expression of concern. He looked at Drake, then at Parsons. He handed bound reports to Parsons and shook his head, disconcerted. "I've seen quite a bit, in all my years on the job, but . . ."

"What is it?" Parsons asked.

Chief Peters folded his arms across his chest. "There was not a ballistics match to Mr. Drake's gun. It appears there was no ballistics evidence to match at all."

"What does that mean?"

"What it means is that we've searched the Fitzsimmons scene and the scene at the conservatory, and there were no traces, none whatsoever, of any gunfire. No gunpowder residue, no bullet casings or fragments, nothing."

Drake listened and observed.

Parsons looked dumbfounded. "How can that be?"

"I don't know," Chief Peters said. "The gun I recovered from Mr. Drake at the conservatory was empty, and there was no evidence of gunfire. Not a trace. It was clean, like it had never been shot."

"Never?"

"It was clean."

Drake didn't blink.

"You do have the dead bodies, right?" Parsons asked.

"We do have the dead bodies. I had the chief medical examiner work on all of them, priority. The report is there."

Parsons leafed through the first two pages and read the summary.

Chief Peters said, "Fitzsimmons was found in his home, in his library, dead in a chair. The cause of death: heart attack. There was a streak of his own blood that ran from his forehead down to the tip of his nose, and a dried blotch on his shirt and sweater. But the medical examiner couldn't find the source. No puncture wound. No marks anywhere on the body. There was no trace of any drugs. He had a heart attack, and died."

"That happens," Drake said.

"It does. We also found a dead man in Fitzsimmons' front hallway, presumably a bodyguard of some sort. He was huge. They ran his prints. Had two priors for aggravated battery. It seems somebody returned the favor this time."

"How did he die?" Parsons asked.

"Bled out from a puncture wound to the throat."

"A knife?"

"No, something with a blunt end. No weapon has been found. Do you know anything about that, Mr. Drake?"

"No sir," Drake said. His keys were in the car. It was a loose end, he realized, and he knew that this would be an opportune time for Chief Peters to pat him down. But he didn't.

"And then there is Detective Hartman. We found him much the same way as Fitzsimmons, dead that is, of an apparent heart attack. In the Lincoln Park Conservatory, lying in the plants. The front of his shirt was soaked with blood, his blood, but again, no open wound of any kind. He also had the same drip from his forehead, like Fitzsimmons, like someone had painted it there." The chief pondered the situation. He shook his head, perplexed. "It makes no sense." Then he looked at Drake, indifferent but hoping for a reaction. He didn't get one.

"And what about Mrs. Mitchell?" Parsons asked.

"Suicide, pure and simple, like her son, but a different approach. She inhaled a high concentration of cyanide gas, enough to stop a charging rhino. We have the inhaler, and there was residue on her fingertips and lips that matched what was found in the inhaler and in her bloodstream. No other prints."

They all looked at each other for a quiet minute.

Parsons looked down at the reports in his hands. "There isn't much for me to do here."

Chief Peters conceded. "I'll let you know if we come up with anything else."

"Please do," Parsons said. "What about Drake?"

The chief reached into his jacket pocket and pulled out Drake's gun. He set the gun down on the table and slid it over in Drake's direction.

Drake took hold of the gun, but the chief did not let go.

The chief leaned in. "Mr. Drake, you are a writer, yes?"

"I am."

"Then I'd like you to take your gun and lock it away so you can focus on your writing . . . and leave the police business to us."

"It would be my pleasure." Drake pushed his chair back from the table and stood up. He holstered his gun and walked around the table toward the door.

"I don't want to see you back here ever again. Not even for a traffic ticket."

"Of course."

Parsons handed the reports to Chief Peters. "Chief," he said then walked out of the room.

Chief Peters rolled up the reports, squeezed them tight with both hands, and again shook his head in disbelief.

"Hey, Chief?" Drake asked.

"Yeah, what is it?"

Drake reached into his pocket and pulled out Sarah's Mitchell's journal. He handed it to the chief.

"What's this?"

"Billy Taylor gave this to me. He had it all along. Sarah Mitchell gave it to him before she disappeared."

The chief held it like it was the Holy Grail, opened it, and read the bookmarked page. "Well, I'll be damned."

"Not you, Chief, but Alderman Mitchell."

"Unbelievable."

"If it's all right, I'll just leave it with you."

"Yeah. Thanks," the chief said, still reading and immersed in the revelations of the journal.

Drake walked past him.

"And I have something for you." Chief Peters reached into the right pocket of his suit jacket then pulled out a closed fist. He opened his hand like a platter, revealing five bullets. "I think these are yours."

Drake said nothing and put out his hand.

The chief handed him the bullets. "Lock those away too."

"I will." Drake put the bullets into his pocket. "Chief, can I ask you a question?"

"Sure."

"Why did you cover for me—the empty gun?"

"You helped me to finally put this case to bed. I couldn't do anything for my own daughter. At least I can do something for Sarah Mitchell. Now she can rest in peace. We all can."

Drake nodded, turned, and left the room.

* * *

The following morning, Chief Peters held a press conference in front of the 18th District Police Station. He stood in front of a crowd of reporters and photographers who were pushing and shoving each other, rudely and in an act of gamesmanship to secure the best spot to get the scoop. A line of police officers created a barrier to the chief.

"If I could have your attention," Chief Peters said.

The crowd quieted.

"I have a statement to make regarding the recent deaths in the Mitchell family."

"Do you have any suspects?" a reporter asked.

A different reporter followed up and asked, "What were the causes of death?"

"Please, if I could have your attention," Chief Peters said, halting them with a raised hand. There was some talking amongst the reporters, and he waited for it to subside. When it was quiet, he continued, "Ten years ago, there was a murder of a young girl in a case that was never solved. My office, in an effort to reduce our inventory of cold, unsolved cases, recently began looking into the murder. The young girl was Sarah Mitchell, the daughter of Senator Jack Mitchell and his wife, Mrs. Clarisse Mitchell."

The reporters talked again amongst themselves. Some barked into phones while others took notes. Cameras clicked and flashed.

Chief Peters raised his hand again and waited until he was the focus of the crowd's attention. "Our own Detective Mike Hartman was the lead investigator on the case. He had a breakthrough after re-interviewing a friend of the girl and recovering Sarah Mitchell's lost journal. As a result of reviewing the journal, we had reason to believe that Alderman Jack Mitchell was involved in her murder. When Detective Hartman stepped up the investigation and put on the pressure, it was more than the Alderman could take. Late yesterday afternoon, in his office, Alderman Mitchell took his own life with a self-inflicted, single shot to the head from his own pistol."

There was more rustling and commotion within the ranks of the reporters. More pictures.

"Detective Hartman effectively unearthed a trail which led us to Mrs. Clarisse Mitchell and the burial site of Sarah Mitchell."

"Where?" someone yelled.

"Her body was recovered from a grave inside the Lincoln Park Conservatory."

Oohs and *ahhs* permeated the crowd.

"Detective Hartman apprehended Mrs. Mitchell at the conservatory, and there was an exchange of gunfire. Unfortunately, and I am saddened to say, Detective Hartman was killed in that exchange. Immediately following that altercation, Mrs. Mitchell took her own life by inhaling a lethal dose of cyanide gas."

A reporter asked, "But she had a gun. Why the cyanide?"

"I don't know, and I am not able to ask Mrs. Mitchell about her preferred method of suicide."

Drake was in the back of the crowd, close to the street. He looked on and listened.

Ray Parsons stood beside him. "*That* is some interesting fiction."

"It sure is," Drake said.

"And no mention of Fitzsimmons."

"He was a nobody," Drake said. "Always was. Same with the bodyguard. There's no point in the chief complicating the situation any further. And he covered for Hartman as only a chief of police could. Look at him. He and his department get to take all of the credit, and Hartman's a hero, taken down in the line of duty, serving his city."

"Does any of that bother you?"

Drake waved a hand and said, "Nah, I wouldn't want it any other way."

"By the way, you promised me that you wouldn't do or say anything without letting me know first."

"Sorry."

"No, thanks for keeping me out of it."

Drake turned to leave.

"I do have one question," Parsons said.

"Yeah?"

"How did *you* end up at the conservatory?"

"I visited the Belden-Stratford Apartments, across the street from where the hand was found. The Mitchells had an apartment there, first when it was a hotel and then again when the hotel was converted to apartments, and it seemed that Mrs. Mitchell spent a lot of time there. She was also on the board of directors of the conservatory. And then there was Fitzsimmons, who had these unusual flowers in his home, and on my last visit to see him, I saw a fresh smear of white powder on his sweater. It was a powder from a rare flower, a vanilla orchid, a flower, I learned, that was on display in the conservatory."

"Unbelievable," Parsons said.

"Yeah." Drake turned and walked away down the street.

"I'll see you around?" Parsons shouted.

Drake looked back and in mid-stride he said, "It's a big city."

* * *

Later that morning, Drake was back in his apartment, sitting at his desk and typing away at his computer. There was a cup of steaming hot coffee on his desk. Black, without a kick.

Drake stopped typing and read back the words he had written.

His mind wandered for just a moment as he thought about Karen and his two beautiful daughters, all of whom were now safe in their house in the suburbs.

He smiled.

He also thought about Billy Taylor and the fact that he had been given a new lease on life, the past finally put to rest. Earlier, on his way home from the press conference, he had stopped by the grocery store to visit Billy. Drake was surprised when he saw him. It appeared that holding on to the journal for all of those years had created quite a burden for him to shoulder. In the short time since he had handed the journal over to Drake, had exorcised it from his control and conscience, Billy had become a changed man with a new outlook on life. He was a different person. Billy was in an aisle, stacking cans, but was doing so with a renewed vigor. He was dressed in new clothes, well-groomed, and confident. Most important, he was happy.

The thought made Drake feel good. He took a sip of coffee then returned to his keyboard, and he worked on his book for the rest of the day.

27

Drake delivered the manuscript for his new book right on schedule, as he had promised and with a day to spare. The editing process was grueling but condensed into a short amount of time, and his book was part of Random House's spring catalog, as they had planned. The book came out of the gate strong because of some positive pre-publication reviews. The publisher had originally decided on an initial print run of five thousand copies, and one week after the release, they decided to print ten thousand more. The publisher was hopeful about the future success of the book. The weekly total sales of print and e-books had grown in the second week, and they felt the momentum was growing and could be sustained for the next two months. With some additional marketing, positive reviews, and publicity events, they were confident they could get Drake's book on the *New York Times* bestseller list, and from there, anything could happen.

Random House and Drake's agent had coordinated a book-signing event at Drake's bookstore to promote the release of his new novel, and while the book had been released just the week prior, Drake was already savoring the fanfare and relishing the promise of a revitalized writing career.

It was a Friday evening, and Karen and his daughters were at the event, along with Scotty and Engel and two hundred interested book readers and buyers. The publicity had been heavy and relentless for weeks throughout the city and the surrounding suburbs, and it was an incredible crowd, more than Drake could ever have imagined.

Drake stood in front of the large crowd, prepared for a reading from his new book. He looked up and out at the people and waited until they noticed and the room became quiet. "This is a story about a character, about a man, who was given a second chance in life. It's about a man who longed to bury the past, but realized that only by truly embracing the past could he carry on into the future. If you don't mind, I'm going to keep my reading brief this evening so I can have the opportunity to take your questions and meet and talk with each and every one of you."

He opened the book and read the short, first chapter. He liked the first chapter the best, felt the introduction of Jack Cannon was enlightening and the action was fast and in-your-face. The audience was quiet and listening intently, and Drake felt he had effectively captured their interest and attention.

At the end of the first chapter, he paused and looked up at the crowd. He said, "Now, I'd like to read for you the passage that ends the book, and I think it is fitting, because the passage is about an ending, but at the same time and more importantly, it is about a new beginning."

Drake opened the book to a marked page. "Jack Cannon

opened the safe in his office with expert care, like he was opening an ancient tomb filled with buried treasure, and removed the wooden box. He lifted the lid and was not surprised at its emptiness. He removed the Colt 1911 from his holster and set the gun into the box, into the formed and velvet-lined recess where the gun usually slept. He stared at the gun for a moment then closed the lid. He put the box back into the safe, closed the safe door, and spun the combination wheel."

Drake paused and looked up from the book. He saw Scotty standing against the back wall, clapping silently.

Drake continued, "Cannon stared at the safe door. He knew the gun would be safe there. And he knew it would stay there. Until next time."

Drake closed the book, and the crowd applauded.

He looked down at the cover and read the title: A FINE LINE: A JACK CANNON NOVEL. He held the book with one hand and used his other hand to feel the raised lettering of the bold title. The letters rose up off the cover, and the feeling of them under his touch made him realize that *he* was rising up once again.

His agent, Barbara, came up onto the stage and stood next to him, clapping loudly and trying to rouse up the crowd. She turned to him and gave him a hug. "Well done, darling." She spoke to the crowd for a minute and explained the procedure for purchasing a book and having it signed.

She led Drake over to a table stacked with books and pens.

Drake stood behind the table, looked out across the room, and saw that the people had left their seats. Barbara's staff members were herding the people into a long line and keeping them company as they waited.

Drake sat down and uncapped a pen.

* * *

Three hours later, the bookstore had cleared. Rita was cleaning up and preparing to close the store.

Karen, Ted, and the girls walked up to Drake to say their goodbyes.

Ted extended a hand. "Congratulations, Drake."

Drake shook his hand. "Thank you, for helping to find Samantha, for helping Karen to take care of the girls. I appreciate it."

"You're welcome," he said and stepped aside.

Drake bent down to hug and kiss his daughters. Kelly hugged him first. "Congratulations, Daddy." She kissed him on the cheek. "You're the best!"

"No, you're the best," he said, and he kissed her on the forehead.

Then Samantha stepped forward. She held both of his hands and looked up at him, beaming and appearing as though she had aged another year, standing taller and more confident. "I told you, Daddy, that everything would turn out just fine."

"Yes, you did. And I owe you one."

Samantha put her arms around his neck and pulled him close. She put her mouth up to his ear and whispered, "And Mom does still love you." She let go of him and stepped back, a huge grin on her face.

Drake looked at Karen.

There was a silent moment between them, one that only

two people who truly care about each other can share, as they looked into each other's eyes.

Ted took the girls by the hand. "Let's go, girls. It's way past your bedtime." They were both grinning, heads turned back and looking at their parents as they walked away.

"Bye, Daddy," the girls said in unison.

"See you soon," Drake said, and he watched them walk away.

Drake turned back to Karen.

They both smiled.

Karen stepped forward and hugged him. Drake didn't want to let her go, but she released her grip and while still in his arms, she leaned back and looked into his eyes. She raised a hand and caressed his cheek. "I'm really proud of you."

They inched closer, as though they might kiss, but stopped at the last possible moment. Drake released his grip on her, and she backed away, blushing and messing with her hair.

"Thanks for coming," Drake said.

Karen, walking backwards, said, "Come by and visit your daughters."

"I will."

She turned and walked away. At the doorway, she passed Engel, and they acknowledged each other with a smile.

Engel walked to the front of the room and approached Drake. "That's quite a novel you've written there."

"I thought you might like it."

Engel said, "Let me know when you're ready to start the next one."

"I will."

Engel handed Drake a gift, a thick rectangle wrapped in simple brown paper.

"What's this?"

"A token of my appreciation, from me and my brother. You can open it later."

They shook hands, and Engel turned and walked away.

"Hold on, I have something for you." Drake reached into his pants pocket and pulled out a ring of keys. "It seems my employment with you has ended. Here's your car back."

"Can you hold on to it and take care of it for me, for a little while? Otherwise, it will just collect dust and rust. And, who knows, something may come up, and you might need it."

"Okay. I'll take care of it."

"Good evening, Mr. Drake."

Drake watched Engel until he reached the far end of the room, entered the elevator, and disappeared behind the sliding cage door. Then, he looked down at his gift.

He removed the paper and was surprised when he looked down at the cover of a book and saw: *DARK CARNIVAL, RAY BRADBURY*. It was the book he had seen while in Engel's library. He opened the front cover and found a note card, which he took out and read.

> *Mr. Drake,*
> *Now we have a relationship.*
> *Sincerely,*
> *Engel*

Rita walked up to him. "That was quite an event, and we sold a lot of books. Congratulations."

"Thank you, Rita, for everything," Drake said, and he hugged her. "You'll close up?"

"Yep."

Drake spun around and looked at his empty bookstore, contented. He walked across the room and yelled over his shoulder, "See you tomorrow." He stepped into the elevator, closed the cage door, and descended to the lower level.

He was back in the game.

* * *

The following morning, Senator Mitchell was alone in his room, sitting in a high-backed chair and staring out the window, glassy-eyed. In his lap was a copy of Drake's new book, which he held in his hands like a bar of gold.

Senator Mitchell caressed the book as though it contained some sacred text. He looked down at the book and studied the cover. His fingers ran over and felt the raised lettering of the title, just as Drake had done, and the Senator, too, had come to a realization: it was over. He opened the front cover, and there was a note card inside. The senator did not know it, but the note card was exactly like the one inside the book that Engel had given to Drake—the same paper texture, color, and weight, the same color of ink, and the same handwriting style.

On this card, however, there was only one sentence:

Thank you for your help.

Senator Mitchell looked up and directed his gaze to the beautiful landscape and the day unfolding on the other side of the thin pane of glass.

The senator smiled.

Acknowledgments

The author gratefully acknowledges the following individuals who were instrumental in the development of this book: Don Evans, Randy Richardson, Ashley McDonald, Renee James, Lisa Lickel, Brian Johnston, Pat Camalliere, Florence Osmund, Lisa Schroeter, Kristin Oakley, Ed Marohn, Roxe Anne Peacock, Marie Becker, Janet Cole, Marssie Mencotti, Julie Halpern, Christine Cacciatore, Christine Cassello, Ed Sarna, Caryn Green, Opal Freeman, Starza Thompson, Charles Kuner, Elizabeth Melvin, Tom Sanderson, and Anson Miller.

About the Author

Dan Burns is the author of the novel, *Recalled to Life*, and the short story collection, *No Turning Back: Stories*. He is also an award-winning writer of stories for the screen and stage. He resides with his family in Illinois and enjoys spending time in Wisconsin and Montana. For more information, please visit www.danburnsauthor.com

CPSIA information can be obtained
at www.ICGtesting.com
Printed in the USA
FFHW021212160519
52493731-57911FF